C000097472

THE DARLINGS OF SOHO

DAVID BARNETT

PANTHA PRESS 2012

LONDON

The Darlings of Soho

Copyright © David Barnett 2012

All Rights Reserved

No part of this book maybe reproduced in any form, by photocopying or by any

electronic or mechanical means, including information storage or retrieval

systems, without permission in writing from both the copyright owner and the

publisher of this book.

ISBN – 13: 978-1479331628

PANTHA PRESS

panthapress@yahoo.co.uk

ACKNOWLEDGEMENTS

To get to this point has taken the input and support of family and friends. Thanks to my parents, Easton and Madge who instilled such a strong belief in learning and self-development. My brother Michael and twin Paul who have been there every step of the way.

Jurgen who inspired this novel.

My friends for being there. Caroline for the feedback and coffee.

I am grateful for the bursary I received in order to study at Chelsea College; the input from classes at City Lit; and the fine-tuning at Birkbeck University.

Love and light,

Dave.

In a moment I can fill

you

with wonder, in the next

a well of despair.

At times thrill you

with

new adventures and

occasionally

a beauty

most

                rare.

PROLOGUE

The streets of Soho are desolate. There is a dense silence hanging in the air like a fog.

People huddle in the small 'Costa' coffee shop on Compton Street. The strong, satisfying smell of coffee wafts through the packed space, it's familiar smell lending normality to an abnormal situation. People lean or sit where they can. Against the chrome counter or wooden balustrades leading down to the cavern like basement. On the red leather upholstered stools lined up by the shop window. They wait and they wait…listening to the radio; listening for news.

A bomb went off at Kings Cross rail station only twenty minutes ago and another has gone off on a bus in Russell Square carrying women, children, brothers, fathers. No one knows where the next one may go off. People have been instructed to stay where they are. Police have cordoned off the centre of London.

'It's like the blitz,' says an elderly lady sitting huddled next to her husband, sipping tea, an ear towards the stainless steel receiver, that has become the only portal to the outside world. Everyone is trying to stay cheerful, buoyant when all that is normal has been decimated. Blown into a thousand tiny pieces. When they breathe the air catches on it's way down. They wonder how and why this destruction is happening.

The Italian manageress with her kind weary face, doles out more free coffee and tea. A young woman pipes up that she shouted at her kids this morning and if she ever gets home she will hug them every day, tell them she loves them. She bursts into tears as she says these last few words. The horror of what is happening cascades like a wave through the group. The lady's tears a reminder of how delicate the thread of life can be.... and yet, as a young man leans across to comfort her with his hand outstretched, the ties that bind them all, in that very moment, seem stronger than anything else. There is a comfort in that. The kind that reassures you; takes away your fear.

Greg was on the Piccadilly and Martina on the Northern line, heading to Kings Cross early that morning. They had arranged to meet for a coffee and croissant at Patisserie Valerie also in Soho. A conventional French cafe situated in the most unconventional part of town; where gay, straight, and all those in between, loved to meet. Greg had some exciting news for Martina. He had made a decision. His heart was racing, his head giddy with love and possibilities.

Martina with her wide red lips, was smiling to herself as she picked up the Metro newspaper next to her in the carriage. She glanced at the watch on her slim sun browned wrist; she was running a little late. She hated being late. A couple more stops and she would be at Kings Cross. If she hadn't stayed over night at Sam's she would have been there by now. A sigh escaped louder than she had expected. The lady opposite her smiled, her brilliant blue eyes framed by black lacquer framed glasses, holding her own copy of the Metro neatly folded on her lap.

Greg was looking up at the tube map above the window of the tube train. Only two more stops. He would have to run up the stairs but he should just make it. He prayed that the train wouldn't get delayed in a tunnel. He didn't want to keep Martina waiting.

Charlie, Greg's boyfriend, was on the mobile calling frantically, trying not to panic. Trying to breathe; to punch the digits on the phone. The telly was on; he had just heard the unimaginable, that a bomb had gone off earlier at King's Cross. Only just pieced together the threads. His mind wasn't working properly. Wasn't taking things in. Greg was meeting Martina somewhere in central today. He had mentioned something about an early start. Something about meeting to discuss a few ideas for end of term. He looked at the phone the network had crashed. There was no contact. The strings of his heart were pulling; he felt an ache. The moments ticked passed. He sat half listening to the telly, half his attention on the phone. Waiting for it to connect.......

CHAPTER 1

Love me fast, love me slow....

Martina whispered the words in her head. Her thoughts seemed to melt; come into focus then turn to liquid again...She raised her slender neck, as she felt her self roll onto her side. Aware that she was caught some where between dream and reality, she stretched out her legs as pleasure rushed to her brain.

Heard herself repeat the mantra...love me fast... love me slow. Was this what it felt like to love without boundaries; to experience herself as she truly was? She could no longer separate mind and body, waking or sleeping, truth or untruth.

Suddenly her eyes opened wide and Martina let out a low groan.

" Damn." The alarm on her mobile was loud and demanding, morning was here, and with it the same feeling of dislocation that she had been experiencing a lot lately. Her arm reached beside the bed to press the disable button on the Motorola key pad.

9

"Damn", She cursed again. Why the wrench every morning? The same frustration waking up? The same dissatisfaction? The questions pounded away in her head, like a dull ache, as she slipped her hands over the top of the smooth, cream satin sheets.

If only she could get this angst or what ever the hell it was, out of her mind – remain in the beautiful light that came just before dawn.

She looked over at Sam, darling sweet Sam still snoring his head off beside her, and wondered in a slightly detached way, if men could ever stay in her life for longer than six months. Darling sweet Sam who was safe and secure, generous and kind; lay there on his back. His pale hairy chest rising up and down. Martina got up quickly and headed for the bathroom. She didn't want to think too much – remember too much of her night before. To want more for herself, someone who already felt so undeserving, was the sure way to madness. So no, she

10

couldn't think too much. Remember too much. Everything was at stake.

As the warm water gushed through the shower, onto her scalp, her mind flooded with images of a stranger.... A seductive stranger with a perfect body and fresh mint teeth. She closed her eyes, straining to see Sam in his place. Sam, the man she wanted to make a go of things with – who knows to marry maybe. The man who had promised to look after her, support her, be loyal to only her.

His job as a bank clerk had meant security (though recent redundancy had upset that applecart.) His large soft body had given her comfort and his words still gave her love. But, and as hard as she tried to ignore it, there was a but; where was the passion? Where was the fire within the relationship? At best, sex with Sam was obliging, the movement in his hips always slight. It seemed he would rather cuddle her than make love. Although Martina loved affection, she also loved sex. The stripped away mystery, the reality, the intimacy. She loved all of it.

Steam had misted up the glass cubicle. She began to massage shower gel into her skin, her mind swimming elsewhere. The spicy, astringent smell of ginger took her even further; her limits dissolving; almost becoming pure sensation. The water now pounding against her face … against the kiss me lips and wide friendly; almost innocent features. She wasn't sure that Sam needed passion to drive him, wasn't sure if he was made like that.

She could see him now in her minds eye holding her on the settee, the way he always did. Smiling with big wet eyes at her. Big wet soppy eyes that promised no more famine, only feast. Round plump cheeks that reminded her of her father. The water stopped as Martina switched the faucet off, aware suddenly that she was running late for college.

Stepping onto the bath mat she glanced into the small narrow mirror on the opposite wall. Curious how a glance is all it takes. Smile lines had etched themselves around her mouth and richly coloured eyes. The pale olive skin around her nose now peppered with small open pores. A couple of gray hairs emerged through the lustrous, wet hair. Her waist though trim was loosing its tightness. Small breasts still looked pert, but how long could she expect to look young when thirty eight was only a couple of months away; and forty round the corner? How long before the maternal bell that still sounded stopped ringing at all? Wasn't that the life plan, find yourself a nice young man and settle down? That was what mum had always said.

Martina rubbed her short hair vigorously before wrapping the thick white towel around her chest. She flicked a comb through her fringe, sweeping the strands over her left ear, in a chic French kind of way and why not she thought; she was more French than British, or at least her parents had been.

Martina was an only child from French parents who met in Paris, but settled in London. Both pursuing careers as actors at a time when London was opening up to what French cinema had to offer. In a way Martina felt she was carrying them within her, their words of affection, of reassurance; that only love could satisfy, could fulfil life. To find it was to find one's purpose.

Both had died in a car crash leaving her, at twenty nine, an adult orphan. She remembered the day that she got the news… the feeling of complete emptiness. Her parents; her anchor to what had been for the most part a happy life, gone; lost in the ether. Then came the strange feeling of moving through what had become her existence, a kind of soup. Not being able to take anything in; just going through the motions of living. Her reality suddenly blurring into unreality; where nothing, not even the existence of a God, any longer made sense.

They had left her the two bedroom flat that she had lived in most of her life. The only material thing tying her to the past.

14

Each Spartan room left no clue that she had a past at all. Everything that she needed was locked away inside of her. Absorbed into every living cell, every muscle, every nuance in the way that she was as a person. Nothing else tethered her.

Going from house to house, job to job, and city to city, meant that their family had moved over ten times within the same number of years – you couldn't afford to become too attached. Acting could be insecure and so you learnt to travel light. Not until she had to re-take her o'levels did her parents make the conscious decision to settle in London. This small two bedroom, regency style flat in the heart of Camden was something her parents had bought when the area was still a place for artisans, and still affordable to those not born into money. God only knew what it was worth now.

Martina's mind came back to the present and her sleepy boyfriend who was now standing in front of her, stark naked. He scratched his short blond hair nonchantly. Looked at her with bleary eyes,

"You don't want to be late on your first day hon ."

"I know, I know," replied Martina, hurriedly pulling on bra and knickers, before dashing into the kitchen to switch on the kettle. There was a time when a morning fumble was welcome or some lazy kissing. But now that her body knew his, not even curiosity could conjure up some kind of interest. What was she to do? Kelly, her closest friend since sixth form and guru to all who knew her, said that she needed to rebalance her space with feng-shui. If that was out of kilter then nothing worked.

Martina looked at the cactus plant on top of the double height fridge. Maybe if she put it out in the hallway it would create better vibes; block any negative energy that may enter via the front door. She tried to remember what else Kelly had said.

"Oh!" Martina rushed in behind Sam who had begun to head towards the bathroom.

"Remember to put the seat cover down when your finished sweetie, want to stop my prosperity being sucked down the loo."

"Your prosperity?" sighed Sam, slightly aggrieved at being asked to change a life times habit. "What's this MY business? I thought we were a couple, not landlady and tenant!?"

"Oh don't start," retorted Martina, "you know what I mean, and anyway it's not as though the extra efforts going to kill you, is it?" She rushed back out to the kitchen before Sam could reply. No time for an argument – she was late.

Her mind flitted to the past just for a second as she stood at the sink, absent-mindedly running the cold tap.

After studying business management at university, Martina had gone onto work in hotel management. And she worked hard at it. Something she had been proud of. But over time enthusiasm had dwindled and her energy with it. A strange dissatisfaction had crept in. A pattern woven at the time of her parents death. Nothing she could put her finger on really, just a growing knowledge that something was changing, and she needed to change with it.

Kelly had suggested over the phone that she should accompany her to a chakra workshop and chant for clarity. "Sweetheart you'll be in rapture", where her words, but Martina wasn't quite sure the world was ready for her brand of chanting and went to see a careers counsellor instead. It was then that returning to college came up as an option. Next thing she knew she had been given an interview at Chelsea College. And an acceptance letter to study interior design arrived on her mat several weeks later. Martina had always enjoyed tinkering with D.I.Y. around the flat, and although Sam had laughed at the crooked tiles in the bathroom, now was her opportunity to see whether there was a future for her in the world of interiors.

"Mmmmmwa," went Martina's lips. "Bi hon, see you tonight."

"Have a good one," smiled Sam, eyes still fuzzy and confused. Suzie closed the door behind her, dashed down the stairs and let the front entrance door slam behind her as she headed for the tube station. The arms on her small silver watch face had reached 9.00 a.m. as she glanced down. She hurried on; thrust her weekly travel card into the slot and went through the gate. Her flat slip-on leather shoes made a clicking sound as she raced down the escalator. She could hear a train as she raced onto the northern line platform.

"Di,di,di." The doors where closing. "Please mind the doors," said an automated voice, "please mind the doors."

Breathless Martina lunged.

CHAPTER 2

Love me fast, love me slow, love all of me. These are the words Greg wants to say to Charlie; to say them aloud as they're doing it there on the bed.

It seems too soon to say these words, though he wants to. He feels that he has waited a long time for Charlie to come into his life and now that he has he wants to tell him everything. No holding back. No wasting another lifetime.

Greg strokes Charlie slowly across the stomach, fingering each individual muscle as they tense under his touch. He admired the discipline to mould such tight abdominals. His fingers thin but strong stroke his lovers middle once more. Carefully he slides one hand over Charlie's, careful not to interrupt the rhythm of their love making. That's what it is…love. They hold each other still – just for a moment – then begin again. Charlie moans; his tone deep and pleasurable. He looks up at Greg, his eyes are bashful and playful at the same time. They kiss, Greg's fingers entwining Charlie's. Again they melt just a little bit more. Their wet lips touch. Greg's lips slightly fuller than Charlie's, less contained, his cheek bones less defined. Charlie's coffee brown skin gleaming under a thin veil of sweat.

It's Greg's turn, he lets out a hushed guttural sound, can't help himself. He wants to show his pleasure. Needs to tell Charlie, "I love it." But they are beyond words. Greg lowers his smooth chest down to Charlie's as their breathing quickens. Their eyelids close as they become pure sensation. And Greg wants to say, I love it – I love you.

They lie next to each other panting, one lean frame against the other. Boom, boom, boom, goes Greg's heart. His manhood is sticky. The room smells of sex.

  "Talk to me," he whispers, " tell me what your thinking." His skin, a golden caramel; rubs against Charlie's stomach…..
wavy dark hair falls against his lovers forehead as he tilts his head slightly, looking away, suddenly shy. The silence hangs over them like a mist, and then….

"That I really like you and that you're incredible."

"You're not so bad yourself." Greg grins, showing slightly crooked teeth, his voice woozy with exhaustion. They've been at it half the night and now it's morning outside.

"Eeeee! Eeee! Eeeee!" A loud siren breaks the moment. An ambulance speeds past, chicaning through the streets; below the third floor apartment.

"I've got to go pee." Greg's voice is a whisper.

"Not yet," begs Charlie quietly, pulling himself up into a sitting position. Greg turns silently, bends his body deliberately, to kiss him on the lips, then leaves the room. He's back in a few minutes, a look of relief across his face. He lays down once more, sliding an arm around his lovers shoulders. And once more they enter the world of the sublime.

As they finally stumble off the bed, sheets all ruffled, it's 4.00a.m. on the clock. They walk into the long narrow hallway of the flat; matt cream walls either side; then into the shower room. Bright white tiles line the walls. A cubicle shower in the corner. Greg loves his flat. It's stark simplicity, grounding him

22

in the face of his own complexity. They rest their towels on the hard pine bench next to the shower before jumping in. They laugh as Greg works soap into Charlie's skin – his hands moving in a circular motion as though it were his own body. Greg's head is dizzy with happiness as he lathers the soap over his lovers' pectorals. He leans into him a little more. The water is heaven. They continue to bathe until the smell of sex is less obvious; less telling.

"Enough," Greg says lazily, his face smiling. He switches the water off and steps out onto the small white cotton rug that lies in front of the cubicle. He begins to dry off as Charlie steps out beside him. Greg can see how similar their bodies look in the tall narrow mirror propped against the far wall. Heady with exhaustion he sits down on the bench, continuing to dry himself hurriedly; his stomach rumbles. Charlie smiles,

"Certainly time for some sustenance." Greg flicks his eyes up to Charlie's; browns mix together.

"You can eat me," Charlie laughs as he kneels down in front of Greg.

"Very corny," Greg allows Charlie to hold his middle, moving his tongue against the inside of his small neat navel. He chuckles, he can't help responding, his towel falls…

*

Greg has often gone for boyfriends similar to himself physically but always completely different mentally and spiritually. He presumed it was the challenge of opposing minds and all that. But this, this was different. He can discuss tantra with Charlie; the dictates and freedoms of karma. He can ramble on for hours, about his favourite books. Another Country, The kite Runner, Venus as a Boy…. Share his most private, most intimate thoughts. And it feels like the most comfortable thing in the world… A bit like talking to a more practical, more grounded version of himself …..it feels great.

It is Monday morning and time for college. To Greg it all seems slightly surreal, slightly strange. Like swimming in a larger ocean. Another chapter in his life is beginning.

After several years of teaching art at Latymer, a secondary school in north London, Greg has decided that it is time to return to the role of student; to have a go at channelling his creativity in a new direction. He has been looking forward to this day for some time but it still feels strange. . .that dance with the unknown.

CHAPTER 3

Slightly breathless, Martina entered the small lecture theatre, scanned the room briefly then dropped herself into a front row seat next to a black guy with a friendly grin.

"Hi," she whispered.

"Hi," He grinned again, "my name's Greg," his voice low and charming, his face interested.

"I'm Martina. God I thought I was late."

"Me too," Greg chuckled quietly. Martina smiled as she turned away. The lecturer, a small thin lady dressed completely in black, came in.

"Welcome to Chelsea college," she announced. Bright red lipstick, and close cropped hair gave her English features a slightly severe look. One that seemed at odds with her smooth, silky, almost too soft voice. The kind of voice that you listened to carefully for fear of missing a note.

"First of all my name is Belinda Evans and I'll be one of your tutors for the course alongside my colleague Ben Chambers who you'll meet later on in the day. Now," she turned around to pick up a wodge of small booklets. Clasping them to her, she moved forward and handed the pile to a pretty looking Japanese lady two seats along from Martina. "Pass these along would you please." She then repeated the action, but this time handing the next pile to an English guy across the isle.

"Okay," she clasped the back of her neck (momentarily smoothing down some unruly hair known only to her) with her right hand; her left hand on her waist, "please study these in your own time," she glanced around the lecture theatre reassuring herself that she had every ones full attention, "as they will give you the outline for the course and the criteria that you will need to meet for each of the modules." A large opal ring on her left hand reflected in the glare of the fluorescent tubes hanging from the ceiling. "Right then, has everyone got a handbook now?" People nodded, a few murmured yes in a rather shy - I don't want to draw attention to myself yet – kind of way. Some muttered no in the back row.

Belinda sufficiently satisfied, then marched over to a projector sitting on a small trolley on the other side of the space. She pulled it into the centre, then turned back to her audience.

"Okay, has everyone got a handbook now?" She paused looking once more at the back row. "Great." Belinda pulled on a lead with a switch. "I'll now show you some of last years work and the sorts of things you'll be expected to cover. Oh, could you get the lights please." She nodded to a female student in her forties sitting nearest the door. "That's lovely." Martina slid down slightly in her seat, ready to be entertained. The projector whirred and up came the first image.

"Wow," everyone murmured.

Twenty minutes later and the bright fluorescent lights where flicked back on. Martina's mind was floating. She let out a slow sigh as if woken from a deep sleep.

"Did you enjoy that?" It was Greg, in a hushed tone.

"Mmm, oh sure," replied Martina quietly, " not sure if I'm ready for this course though. Compared to what we just saw, my drawing looks like a four year olds. Greg chuckled.

28

"God you think you've got worries?" He rolled his eyes upwards. Martina was in stitches - she laughed.

"I think maybe someone should share the joke." It was Belinda looking slightly fierce.

The lunch hour was the opportunity for Martina to visit the Student Services office, up on the third floor. Although she had some savings they weren't going to last the year and Sam clearly wasn't going to turn into some sort of sugar daddy or proverbial knight in shining armour over night. No matter the latent fantasies she had once toyed with. Or at least not anytime soon... so she needed some sound financial advice. She knocked on the grey office door.

"Come in," said a female voice.

"Hi," said Martina entering the small neat office, feeling a little flustered, not used to asking for help from strangers; not used to asking for help full stop. She glanced over at a notice board carefully covered with small squares of information and pictures that suggested that help was in reach. The air smelt mildly of lemons and clean laundry.

"Please sit down and tell me how I can help. My name's Juliet, yep as in Romeo." She laughed. Her face warm and friendly. Martina begun to feel at ease. Her shoulders relaxed.

"Martina, nice to meet you." She shook hands before sitting down on an institutional, navy blue chair. The tight red roll neck she had on felt too close in this room. "I've come to find out about financial advice." She offered.

Juliet listened intently. Martina felt that what she had just said had been rather feeble, and she could at least have been a little more original.

"Mmm sure, tell me a little about your circumstances," Juliet's tone was sympathetic and even. Her face full of understanding.

This was the sort of person Martina felt she could tell her problems to, life story to, safe in the knowledge that she could understand. Make things alright again. A bit like some kind of surrogate mother. A bit like how her mother used to make her feel when she was a little girl. The way she scooped up her emotions and carried them safely to dry land. Her heart muscle

30

gave an involuntary ache as her train of thought carried her along. Martina wanted to tell her about how boring her life now seemed, how droll, how scary; how she wanted kids but not with Sam, how the early morning dreams that had begun to slide in beside her, were becoming the only real constant in her life. And if it weren't true it would be bloody hilarious. But no – Juliet probably didn't need to know quite so much about her circumstances.

She started by telling her that her savings were running extremely low and that she had no idea as to how she was going to manage....she had simply taken a leap of faith coming on this course.

Twenty minutes later, Martina left Juliet's clean, efficient office with a form to fill in for the access fund. Her life still precarious ... still hanging on a wish and a prayer.

CHAPTER 4

Sat on a high backed chair, in front of a flickering candle, Greg emptied his mind of the day's events. Observed them as they drifted up, one by one. His eyes closed but his mind open. The rhythm of his breath was slow and even. He could see Martina. Hear the conversation they had in the canteen. It was nice to have made a friend so quickly. There was a hard determination to Martina but also a fragility; a sensitivity that reminded him of himself. Greg's breath continued to slow, only just perceptible against the silence, almost still. His eyes suddenly flicked open. Time was up. The lit wax in front of him, burned bright, casting flickering shadows onto the white plastered walls. His hands clasped together he began to pray.

"Thank you God for the blessings that you brought to me today. " his voice a tiny whisper. "Please continue to look after my mother, my brother Bailey, and Leoni my sister. Thank you for blessing me with Charlie. I love you. Amen."

He padded over to the table in front of him and blew out the candle. Then into the lounge hardly making a sound as his thick cotton socks cushioned each step. Erica Badu's, Sun and Moon, played in his mind as he rifled through his c.d. collection.

"Found it," he grinned. Switching on the midi system Greg inserted the disk. The small flat Sony speakers either side of the room sounded like base bins as Erica's sweet, sultry tones filled the flat; defying anyone not to succumb to the magic that is 'Sun and Moon'. Greg started crooning away – feeling relaxed in his black silk shirt, cool against his skin; and black linen trousers that flapped like a sail as he walked. Paul Sebastion cologne wafted on the air. He was cooking dinner for Charlie tonight and he wanted to create mood.

Dimming the lights in the lounge, he made for the small kitchen, with it's clean white units and brushed steel cooker.

"All night long," he sang. Laying a rectangular block of wood onto the work surface, he began chopping onions. Pasta tonight he thought, nice and simple. His mind wondered just for a moment. "Damn!" he screamed as blood gushed from a deep cut at the end of his thumb. "Damn, damn, damn!" Running the cold tap on full he relaxed a little; the cold chill taking away some of the initial pain, numbing it slightly. His eyes surveyed the damage as a hard throbbing started where the numbness had been. White flesh stared back at him through a thin split. "Hmmm." Could be worse he thought, reaching for a paper towel, then wrapping his thumb tightly, "at least I've still got a thumb." He Dashed into the shower room for a band-aid, misjudged his step, tripped over the rug and fell against the gleaming white porcelain sink. There was a dull thud followed by a heavy silence...

The air itself felt heavy as Greg sat there on the hard shower room floor blank and transfixed. Just there looking at the tiles. Arm outstretched he had saved himself from a full blow to the head and had only glanced it instead. But his head swam, why was this happening to him? Were the fates conspiring to ruin his evening completely? Was every happy occurrence to be marred by mishap and misadventure? There was the negative spiral again pulling him in. He stopped himself, drew back. He pulled himself up using the rim of the sink for support. Anger in his gut rose up violently.

"I don't believe it," his voice was high pitched and shrill, " Bloody rug!" He picked it up, then flung it down, as if unsure whether to keep it or get rid of it. He berated himself. "Where was the calm he had found only a short while ago, a moment ago there in the other room? Maybe this served as a lesson to him. Perhaps that was it. He had become complacent. He would strengthen his resolve; take this as a marker on the road to his salvation.

Ding-dong. The doorbell went. His mind jolted back to the time. He glanced at his watch, 7.30 p.m. Bang on time as usual. That was Charlie.

"Hi gorgeous," said Greg opening the front door, the kitchen towel still wrapped around his thumb, "I'm the walking wounded," he continued, holding out his throbbing digit.

"Oh baby what have you done?" Charlie hugged his partner to his chest slightly squashing the desert he had brought against Greg's back. "Ah let's see." Releasing Greg he gripped his wrist scrutinising the cut thumb. "Well I think you'll live." He smiled, his expression teasing.

35

"Are you sure doctor; that was a near death experience you know." Greg's tone churlish.

"Poor Greg." They both laughed out loud and headed back to the shower room, Greg now leaning on Charlie's shoulder, limping slightly in his role as patient. And Charlie clutching his boyfriend's waist firmly with his left hand, whilst still holding the desert in the other. They entered the room.

"Right lets find you a plaster," he announced releasing his waist before, rifling through the medicine cabinet.

"It's stopped bleeding now," Greg's eyes looked playful. He pulled at Charlie's shirt sleeve, landing a kiss on his lips.

"Hey," giggled Charlie, "that's a quick, mmwa recovery." Greg pressed his lips once more to his lover's; thoughts of the dinner, pasta, and sauce, lost in the moment. This brief space of time that was so divine. Desert fell to the floor with a quiet thud. No one was listening.

*

The following morning Greg woke up to the shrill pitch of his alarm clock. A sculptural timepiece balanced on a plinth next to the bed, his high backed chair beside it. He shook Charlie,

36

"Wakey, wakey sleepy head or else you'll be late for work."

"Mmm," mumbled Charlie pulling Greg to him. Greg snuggled up to his boyfriend and gave him a kiss on the neck. They lay there just like that, Greg's lips on his lovers neck, for what seemed ages. The clock buzzer sounded again, it's snooze control kicking in.

"Come on Charlie or you'll be late, the shop won't open itself." Greg started stroking his hair as he feigned sleep. "Charlie," he called playfully. He giggled, raised his head and planted a kiss on Greg's cheek.

"Morning." His voice a bit throaty. Greg knew this was code for I'm really getting up now. End of play.

He watched his naked body as he slipped from the covers. Watched him, easy within his skin; each muscle defined and unashamed.

Charlie managed a small bookshop, Henry's, on the Camden High Street, selling second hand and rare books. Although the pay wasn't great and the hours sometimes unsociable, he loved the contact it gave him with the public. And he loved books.

37

The feel of the shop was undeniably traditional but with a modern twist. A nineteen forties brown leather armchair that smelt of age and old shoes, sat in the corner next to a modern up lighter. Traditional wood bookshelves stood laden with books of obvious antiquity; a laptop propped open on a table next to it to convey a sense of the oblique. It was in the shop that Greg and Charlie first met. The first time that Greg smelt that strange combination of Cedar wood and citrus that always seems to be in the air.

Greg wasn't sure, even now what it was about Charlie that had struck him first. Not quite sure when the connection had happened. If it was the moment he caught sight of his warm brown eyes that smiled hello, as he had entered the shop; or the gorgeous upturned lips that had said hi, before they opened. Or the slightly blemished skin that took away nothing. The faint smell that said I'm a man. Or maybe it was all of these things. The things that go unsaid.

The snooze alarm sounded again. Greg was pulled from his thoughts and back to the present. He stretched his arms up, over his head before leaving the warmth of the bed. He turned the alarm off, slipped into his bathrobe and then trotted off to the kitchen to put the kettle on. Heard himself humming something unrecognisable, in an out of body kind of way; caught up in the moment, simply happy to be.

CHAPTER 5

"Honey I'm cold, be a sweetheart and get another blanket from the airing cupboard, for me please." Martina had been lying next to Sam for some time unable to sleep. Her nose streaming constantly; the little bedside clock screaming goodnight to the restless couple, to no avail. "Achoo," Martina sneezed, "Achoo!" Not a good sign she thought . "Thank you Sam." He threw a thick blue woollen blanket across the bed, adjusting each corner to make sure it fitted neatly.

"I'll get you some hot Ribena , shall I darling?" He looked concerned.

"That would be great, thanks," She sniffed. He padded out again in his long, black towelling dressing gown, looking a bit like a boxer, the hood slung over his head.

This was a man of consideration, kindness, loving...Martina's mind was spinning. How could she give him up? For goodness sakes how could she? And yet how could she allow things to stay the way they were; her energy being slowly sapped? A cycle tyre with the smallest puncture can never last the journey she told herself, someone has to fix it.

"Achoo!" She sneezed again, but this time more forcefully. Her nostrils burned with a sensation that ran down into the back of her throat. She reached for a box of tissues beside the bed and blew hard.

Sam padded back into the bedroom, a steaming mug in hand.

"Here you go sweetie, take a sip of that." Martina sat up smiling weakly, resting her head against the red velvet headboard; it's unusual height giving the room a feeling of luxury. She took a sip from the mug before placing it on the glass side table next to her. She sighed, deflated, the clock glaring at her – 1.15a.m. on it's face. With college in the morning and an interview with Mc Kay's consultancy for Sam, this was not great news. Sam's eyes were filled with concern as he climbed back into bed, kissing his partner on the forehead. "Is that a little better M?" he whispered affectionately, "talk to me." He continued whispering, "Your eyes look unsure, what's up?" Martina looked away quickly, uneasy about being caught unawares, but then that's what she had always loved about

Sam, there was no hiding, no pretence, no mind games.

"It's you and me darling," her voice sounded strained – about to crack. She glanced at Sam's eyes, pools of warm water about to spill over. She looked away. "It's not working anymore, is it?" Her voice sounded final, defeated in some rather sad way. Sam's voice was low but steady,

"What can we do to put things right M, I'm willing to try if you are?" Martina looked into his face once more, holding his eyes this time. Looking to see if she could find a fire burning gently somewhere behind the rock pools that would love you forever.

That night they talked and talked, and talked. They would perhaps make it to the next dawning, to the next place of dry land …but for the moment they had an emotional sea to cross over…. An ocean that spanned both past and present.

Martina could hear the bitterness in her words, the sadness as she described her years of instability. Always moving as a child from one place to the next. Sam clung to her like he had never clung before. He a grown man cried; cried shamelessly; openly; needed her to see his pain; to lessen his burden; to caress him; to sing sweetly in his ears; to remind him of what it was like to be young again. Unburdened by harsh realities.

*

The following morning Martina glided along the streets of Chelsea, buoyant with hope. A stride in her step. Of course she was tired, really tired, but it was a good tired. She entered the large lecture theatre five minutes late. Belinda glared.

"Sorry," offered Martina hastily, moving toward a space Greg had saved for her in the front row.

"Right," said Belinda, bright red lipstick shining against her skin, "please remember that we start 9.30 a.m sharp and don't have time to repeat things for late comers." She glared at Martina once more. Her narrowed eyes a sign of her imposing control. It was primary school all over again. "Now," announced Belinda, "you've had a week at the college and a chance to get to know each other a little, so today we'll get you started on a short assignment." Martina wasn't sure of the link here but tried to stay focused. "You've all got sketch books for

43

today, yes?" Belinda continued, not waiting for or expecting comment. "We want you to sketch the shapes and geometry that make up specific monuments and buildings within the central London area, the names of which I shall give you in a moment." She waved a piece of A4 paper over her head. "We," she looked at Ben sitting in his black loafers and matching black suit for affirmation, "would like you to please think about textures and materials using colour as a medium….as your sounding board. Okay Ben will read out the groups and the monuments that you will visit." She looked over to Ben once more. He pulled his mad curly hair back, away from his face, before rising to address the crowd. Martina smiled unconsciously, she liked Ben. In his slightly eccentric way he was charming. His features soft and fair. His manner unhurried. She glanced at Belinda, her shrewd features set, waiting for defiance. She felt a little worried as to the future of their student – teacher relationship. More like teacher – child judging from Belinda's present attitude. She cringed inwardly. Ben rattled off the names.

That evening Martina returned home late, much later than the usual, having stopped at Starbucks, for a coffee with Greg and then Tesco Metro for some groceries. The flat was in darkness, except for a trail of tea lights leading into the bedroom. Soft jazz wafted out in a blanket of seduction. She felt weak and giddy, and girlish all in the same breath.

"Hi Sam!" she called. Her heals clicked against the bare stripped wood floor.

"In here!" called Sam from inside the bedroom. Martina dropped her bag before ambling into the candle lit interior of the room. It was decadent, the number of candles lit around the room was magical. Sam grinned as he grabbed her around the waist; pulling her down onto the bed as he did so.

"Is this passionate enough for you?" He teased her ear with his tongue. It tickled, made her weak. She drew back giggling, but wanting to cry.

"Wow, Sam you've …well I'm not sure what to say…. you make me wonder what I've done to deserve you." She kissed him on the lips – her heart melting.

"I love you," he whispered , his voice tender, "I'll do everything in my power to make you happy M. I'd give you the stars if I could." He smiled and her heart melted a little bit more.

"I love you too darling…" Martina's voice trailed off as she lowered her face onto Sam's chest, holding him there, squeezing him to her, feeling the rhythm of his heart beating up and down.

"By the way, I got the job with Mc Kay's. Your now looking at, financial consultant to the stars." They both laughed.

"I knew you'd get it," said Martina softly, her warm breath against his chest. She felt safe, the child within secure once more. For all her apparent independence and self-refinement, she still needed these simple moments, to share in the glow from another human being. Still needed to feel protected from time to time. She pressed herself against him all the more as the woody scent that he was wearing took her back to another time and place. The place she was cradled in her father's arms her mother watching over her…the place she called Eden.

That night the love was passionate. Both Martina and Sam pouring themselves into each other to the point of exhaustion…

"Come on," said Martina finally, " we've got to eat."

"Five more minutes?" Sam continued to run his fingers through her hair as they lay there, still holding. His skin hot against her own. She relaxed once more, brushing her cheek against his. Sam's stubble began to chaff but she said nothing.

*

Three days later Martina was sketching squares, circles and rectangles into numerous configurations. Hurriedly pasting on acrylics and pastels in a flurry of activity. There were only five of them in the studio today, the rest of the group doing their own thing with the study day.

"Let's see," Greg leaned over her shoulder. Her bright orange sweat top blending in with the last flickers of summer. " That looks nice," Greg's voice sounded less up beat today, a little tired. "I am so, so behind," he continued, "Belinda's going to go catatonic if I don't pull my finger out."

"Oh Sure," Martina's voice was teasing. "She loves your work. How was it she described your drawings…beautifully

47

simple, Die-Stiel like in their construction." She lifted her eyes towards the ceiling. "Jammy so and so." They laughed. Greg rubbed her affectionately on the shoulder instinctively, just for a moment. But in that moment she felt a charge, energy, something shift inside un-expectantly. For a split second the thoughts in her mind were scrambled.

"All I get is fine." Martina's mind was back in gear as though nothing had happened, but something had. Her heart was pounding. She continued to work, her head down…leaving the strands of her hair to slip from behind her ear.

Her movements were no longer her own.

What had happened here today?

CHAPTER 6

Yes Greg did have girl friends in the past, but nothing serious. Never knew sex with a man until the age of twenty three and that was with a guy called Viv. Someone he met in a cinema on Tottenham Court Road. It was an initiation of a kind. There had been no caring feeling between them, no belonging. All attention was centred on the act. It seemed to go on for ages. Everything becoming a blur in his mind, a mirage; just raw sensation. Nothing seemed clear. And then it was over.

"What are you thinking?" Asked Charlie aware that his boyfriends mind was else where. No longer focused on the television.

"Oh stuff," answered Greg vaguely. Charlie sidled up to him on the white and blue striped settee squeezing his partner's thigh knowingly.

"Hey do you think she's attractive?" Charlie's head now rested in Greg's lap, eyes still fixed on the television screen; an image of Madonna cavorting in the back of a limo with two girls; lots of lipstick and attitude.

"Yeah I think so, " answered Greg, "She's not afraid to express herself and that in my book is attractive. There was a pause. "People may be fortunate with their looks but I reckon that their thoughts play a big part in how much they actually shine…Mmmm….and you good looking must be thinking lovely thoughts. Greg bent his neck downwards and kissed Charlie on the cheek; his lips rasping against stubble.

"You charmer you. Right come on you," he said, suddenly raising himself up, "how do you fancy coming for a walk with me up by the park? It's a beautiful night." His voice sounded deep, gravely; his eyes wide with excitement. Greg loved that about Charlie, the impulsiveness, the fire. He winked at him as he hauled himself off the settee. Charlie winked back, before traipsing into the bedroom for both shoes and jacket.

Greg switched off the T.V. and followed him into the bedroom; sat on the bed and began pulling on a pair of fawn Timberland boots. The air was beginning to get a little bit chilly now as the daytime hours were decreasing. He pulled a black bomber jacket from his wardrobe. Charlie waited on the edge of the bed. As Greg turned, he admired him sat there in the smokey dim light, poised like a panther.

"Greg come on will you," Charlie launched himself from the bed impatient now to be out.

Within minutes both of them were out of the door and walking hand in hand up a slight incline which lead them onto a small park. The sky was clear, the stars unobstructed by roof tops. They paused to look up.

"Wow," sighed Greg clutching his lover's hand tighter, "Just wow, look at that sky. The stars look so close, so bright. Charlie rested his head on Greg's shoulder saying nothing. His hand felt warm in the chill of the night. There was a silence. Both of them standing there in awe of it all. Each star a blazing light. Charlie resting on Greg.

Greg was the first to break the silence.

"They're beautiful just like you buddy," his voice low, his shoulder steady. Charlie raised up his head,

" That's the most romantic thing anyone has ever said to me," his voice slightly strained. He started to say something else but stopped. A lone figure, leading a small dog passed them by, head down, not looking up, not looking round, just not interested. Greg and Charlie walked on, burning bright. At one with a world still turning.

*

Saturday morning saw Greg at 'Mr Toppers', the barbers on Moor Street. A pungent street smell mixed with perfumes and hair wax. It was busy as usual with the young trendy clientele preparing for a night out on the town. Peacocks, preening and cruising for talent at the same time. Jez, a well built latino, already had someone sitting in the traditional, red leather barbers chair, when Greg entered the shop. Bright orange and blue walls blew away any last cobwebs clinging to the day. Retro funk gave a lively vibe to the place. He sat down on one of the black wooden stools lined up against the wide shop window, whilst observing Jez in the bank of mirrors that had been hung in front of each station. Admiring the tribal tattoo that curved over the right side of his angular face, then down the side of his neck, before disappearing beneath his shirt collar.

"How are you ?" asked Jez smiling and cutting at the same time.

"Good," smiled back Greg, " You?"

"Yep, always good me. Isn't that right Keith?" His question directed at his workmate. They laughed a private laugh.

"Sure thing," answered Keith finally.

Jez spun the chair with his gym chiselled client still firmly fixed to it.

"All done," he announced, "want to see the back where I striped you? Just kidding," He chuckled, holding the mirror up for him to see for himself. He nodded cool approval before releasing himself from the chair and apron in one smooth movement.

"The usual mate," Jez held out his palm and money exchanged hands.

Greg turned around, momentarily distracted by two colourful drag queens striding past the window arm in arm screaming on top of their voices, in order to get the attention of someone they knew further up the road.

"Ready for me," Greg smiled launching himself up from the stool, as he turned back. He slipped his black bomber jacket off, put it on a hook, then landed in the chair. Jez draped the barber's apron over his red Levi's t-shirt.

"Number one all over?" asked Jez knowingly.

"You got it," smiled Greg into the mirror in front of him, "sorry to be so predictable but it's the only constant in my crazy, crazy life." They both laughed a deep hearty laugh. The kind that is from deep down in the belly.

"Hey did you start that course of yours?" enquired Jez whilst running the razor over Greg's head.

"Yep."

"And how's it going?"

"Pretty good," Greg grinned looking into the mirror once more.

"All arty is it? You guys have life too easy … just one big doss."

"If only," quipped Greg. "This months been real intense and we get our first assessed project next week, so the pressures on." His voice went up an octave. They laughed.

The door swung open. In walked a petit well made up woman, swinging a small Indian handbag in one hand and a large paper boutique bag in the other. Her hips swivelled with the practiced effort of walking in high heels.

"Hi darling," she smiled looking at Keith, "Alright?"

"Hi sweetheart."

Jez looked over at the woman, he smiled.

"Alright?" he asked in a heavily put on cockney accent.

"Hiya Jez," She spun around again to face Keith.

"Just come to find out if you want something special for dinner tonight as I'm in a good mood," She held up the evidence of a productive shopping spree, " then again if you want to come round Jez, I'll get something in cheep and cheerful. She spun around once more. Straight blond bleached hair sweeping her face.

"Oh charming," said Jez looking slightly peeved.

"Oh you know what I mean," she piped up quickly. Jez tried to force a smile.

"Anyway I'll get Shirl to come round if your coming, have a bit of a get together. She'll be up for some company. You know she's single now?" She winked in the mirror at Jez. Greg was suddenly reminded of when he was single ... that great sea of desert; he had learnt patience then ..... those lonely days made busy.

"Single, what happened to her boyfriend then?" Jez asked, eyes alight.

"Hmm, thought that would get your attention. She and Larry had a big bust up because, and can you believe this ... she came home after a sixteen hour shift and he expected her to cook him dinner! Can you believe it!?"

Jez looked thoughtful,

"After a sixteen hour shift you wouldn't have thought making him a bit of dinner would make much difference." The whole shop burst into laughter. Greg enjoyed visiting the shop just for this reason. He always felt a part of something here. A community where no two people were the same but knew how to celebrate that. Life felt great.

*

That night saw Greg and Charlie walking hand in hand along the brightly lit Charing Cross Road. Brightly coloured restaurants and cafes screaming for your attention. They had decided to take a chance and see what was on at the Prince Charles cinema just behind the main Soho drag. Another couple held hands in front of them. Greg smiled. It was nice to see others in love. The air was charged above the throng. There was a feeling of expectation, the promise of a great night out in the city. People eager to get to where they were going as they excused and pressed their way forwards. Cologne and cigarettes mingled with the smell of onions being fried at the burger stands lining the roadside.

"Do you realise this will be our first movie together?" asked Charlie "That's like our first mile stone." He turned his head to glance at Greg. His lips pulled into a wide smile.

"I know, " chuckled Greg, "it's ama.." He didn't finish his words.

"FUCKING QUEERS!" shouted a pair of youths, one black, one white, hanging out of the back of a double decker bus. The bright red paint blurring as it sailed passed. "FUCKING QUEERS!" they repeated as their voices trailed into the distance. Their poison spilled.

Greg's head snapped round, for a split moment he wanted to retaliate, do something in defence of their freedom. Show his revulsion against such rabid ignorance. As he recoiled, he felt like telling those sympathetically glancing in their direction not to concern themselves; not to give more attention than necessary to something so sickening; that he already knew what it was like to be called ugly, violent names in public. Have your dignity assaulted in the streets. He knew only too well.

This wasn't the first time. Only then it had been about skin.

He spun round. Charlie had stopped, a stunned look on his face. As though he had been physically attacked. A rabbit in headlights with nowhere to hide.

58

"You okay?" Greg's voice edged with concern. The mood only moments earlier so completely spoilt, soured.

"Sure I'm fine. What ass holes!" His temper fired. "Just when you think as a society we've progressed; moved forward (He paused). We're in the fucking millennium for Christ's sakes." He was breathing hard.

"Okay, calm, deep breaths." Greg's manner was half serious, half joking. He squeezed Charlie's hand and took him into the nook of his shoulder. "Look we're okay. Try not to let it get you down. We can't let bigots like that win, can't let them lower us to their level. Can we?"

"Yeah…I guess your right," replied Charlie in a tired-weary voice. "I'm just sick of this, sick of… ". His voice dropped. Greg slowed down to face Charlie; him and Charlie in their own private bubble. Oblivious of the crowds moving past them.

"Go on?" His voice was gentle, imploring him to continue.

"When I was in college I fell in love….for the first time." He pulled away from Greg as though being suddenly rejected; cast away from the arms of the man he loved.

59

"What happened?" asked Greg, unphased. Charlie looked into his face searching, unsure of how to proceed.

"Oh ....in a nut shell someone saw us kiss and by the next day nearly everyone we knew was treating us like dirt, calling us faggots behind our backs." Charlie looked away. It was awful. I stopped seeing him shortly after that. I just felt so weak Greg...cowardly really." Tears welled up on the surface of his eyes; brimming against the edges. Him holding them back. Them escaping anyway. "Why do people have to be so nasty," he gulped, "so ....fucking nasty?" His voice nearly a whisper. He looked at Greg.

"I know, human nature's queer like that." Greg smiled. A bittersweet smile. Humour his only defence. Charlie half smiled then looked away, eyes shining. The tension suddenly gone. Greg took him in his arms; patted the small of his back in that reassuring way that parents do; as if to say it's all okay again. He sighed inwardly, realising in that moment just how much he loved Charlie; loved him for trusting him, for revealing himself to him, for letting him in. They walked on. This time it seemed best to rest a hand around each other's shoulders. Reducing the risk of further abuse, if only for this one night.

They arrived at the cinema and 'A Wonderful Life' was showing, which seemed poetic somehow. So Greg and Charlie went in although they had both seen it already.

"I love this film," said Greg once they had found their seats.

"Me too." Charlie reached for his partner's hand in the semi-darkness. Greg squeezed back, anchoring his other hand on a bucket of popcorn between his legs. The film titles came up and Charlie snuggled into Greg, resting his head against his shoulder. The guy next to them spun around in his seat, glaring in the now pitch dark, only the screen illuminating his eye balls. Greg turned away. He wasn't going to give his night away. He was there with his lover and that was all that mattered. Not the past or the future - just this moment.

Greg meditated that night, watching his breath, his stomach moving in and out. Saw the evening's events like a videotape being played over, but without the sound. He watched and let it go. He prayed hard that night, eyes shut tight against the candle light; prayed hard for a better world. He felt his mind travel to that place between heaven and earth, where the spirit dances and only love sings.

CHAPTER 7

"Come on Sam or else we'll be late." Martina pulled the straps of her long slinky, red dress over her shoulders as she stood in the front of the wardrobes mirrored front. The room's simple decadence an echo of her good taste. It was Friday evening and both her and Sam had been invited to a birthday dinner at a newly opened restaurant and bar on Frith Street, just around the corner from Soho Square. The birthday boy, Christian, was an old college friend who she had kept in touch with over the years.

"How's this?" asked Sam holding up a narrow striped tie with alternating stripes of silver and black.

"That says style. You'll look a million dollars."

"That's what we like to hear." Sam grinned into the mirror his girlfriend stood in front of. She smiled back, admiring their reflection; him in his black velvet suit, her in the red velvet dress. He quickly knotted his tie as Martina paused to peck him on the cheek.

"Right which perfume?" she asked spinning around , Channel or Obsession?"

"Oh I think.." his voice trailed off. Martina pulled her mouth into an inane expression.

"What?" said Sam trying to sound incredulous, "I don't know do I?" They're both fantastic." She picked up a small bottle of Channel from the elegant mirrored dressing table and pumped the nozzle. It's subtle scent filling the room.

"Right that's me ready." She spun around again snatching a small vintage purse off the bed and a matching, pillar box red, velvet fitted jacket. The jacket lining, a shocking pink.

"Me too," Sam took Martina's hand and walked towards the front door.

"Mmmm, you smell great." She squeezed his hand pulling him closer, "Sure we haven't got time for a quickie?" Her tone was teasing. Sam chuckled,

"You are insatiable , and no we don't have time." He held the door as she stepped out. The perfect gent she thought to her self, even if spontaneity is a foreign concept. She couldn't help smiling. "What are you thinking?" asked Sam.

"No-thing," she emphasised "thing" in a teasing tone of voice, a smile still on her lips.

*

The 'Catacombs' true to its name was a basement venue. As they climbed down the steep wooden stairs Martina noticed a clock projected onto the stark white wall ahead; it read 8.30p.m. She relaxed a little, they were on time.

The space was well lit with modern down lighters ; a long glass bar against one wall gave a contemporary feel to the space. Low tables in white ash complemented high backed iron chairs. An infusion of urban jazz completed the ambience. Martina looked around for Christian and spotted him at a table near the back of the seated area, with Kelly and some other mutual friends. A small grand piano sat closed a few feet away.

"Hi Christian." Martina gave him a hug. "Mmmwa went her lips against his left cheek, "Happy birthday. For forty you look great. It's about time you caught up with the rest of us." She laughed.

"Caught up!" exclaimed Christian taking the bait, "Let's see now you're still a mere thirty seven and I'm catching up in your world?"

"Don't forget you have to allow for the fact that I'm an old soul," said Martina incredulous, "isn't that right Kelly?" She swung around to smile at Kelly who was, chatting with the rest of the party. With a large clear crystal around her neck and a light blue satin number clinging to a disciplined body, she looked suitably serene.

"That's right darling," she stood up to kiss her friend on both cheeks, " Oh and is this the lovely Sam that we've heard so much about?" Her bright blue eyes sparkled under the lights. Martina hoped that her friends would like him…. harmony was so important to her …. Sam seemed a little sheepish standing next to her; she squeezed his hand for reassurance.

"Oh Sam, Kelly, Kelly, Sam." They shook hands before Martina formerly introduced everyone else. She couldn't be sure what impression her friends had of Sam, but she felt that things had gotten off to a promising start.

"Would you like a drink sweetheart?" asked Sam minutes later.

"That would be great." She felt a swell of affection as she smiled at Sam, his eyes smiling back with their little boy vulnerability.

" I'll surprise you."

"Promises, promises, Martina's lips glinted under the lights, deep shades of purple eye shadow, smoky against her eyelids. She felt like a young school girl again, the excitement and expectancy; teasing the boy she had made friends with; the one who's privates she had wanted to see after swim class. Sam returned with two small glasses filled with a pale blue liquid. The top of each glass had been lit and a blue flame burnt furiously.

"Right then," announced Sam as he sat down, placing one of the glasses in front of his partner with a straw, "suck it down in one." He grinned.

"Gees, what is that called?" Martina's kept her tone playful. She was no drinker, but she wanted to please him, and would take his lead.

"Fire starter." Sam's teeth looked white and even, the same familiar smile. "Come on after three." He took his own straw and placed it into the glass in front of him. Conversation on the table had stopped as everyone looked on. Kelly pursed her lips, curiosity etched a line in an otherwise smooth forehead. Martina turned her attention back to her glass. A part of her wishing that she had eaten before leaving the flat.

"One, two, three." They sucked.

She could feel her cheeks burning, the alcohol vapours rising to the back of her throat, out of her nose. She kept going. It felt great to let go. A flame lit in her stomach. She felt a rush.

"Yeah!" yelped everyone as she lowered the glass to the table. She knew that it wouldn't be long before her head started spinning. The night seemed to be hurtling towards a destination unknown.....

"You okay M?" Sam was giggling, teasing her, touched a finger tip to her nose. She rested a hand on his thigh to steady herself, anchor herself to some semblance of reality. She opened her mouth to say something but the words came out slurred.

"Cad yous orders us some foo…od please Sam?"

"Sure, feeling a little tidley are we?" He laughed. His own words still under his control.

"Kelly tell everyone about that time you had that snog with your cousin Richie." Martina had lost control of the button that say's stop now – warning. Kelly looked mortified, then embarrassed, the smile erased from her face.

"Martina your hysterical darling, God someone get her a sip of water, please." Some composure was quickly returning, as was her poise.

"Hey I've got an idea," Christian piped up, desperately trying to bring the party back to him, "let's all dive round mine and really party!" He scanned the table for confirmation; some winked knowingly, others nodded. Martina did none of these things, just reiterated,

"foo..ood."

"It's okay Martina, plenty of food at mine." He stood up, "Sam do you want to grab her coat? You guys can ride with me and Kelly, Richie and Del can carry the rest, let's go." Christian pulled on a dark blue blazer as he made for the door.

Martina felt her senses returning as she sat inanely munching tortilla chips dipped in some kind of salsa, that Christian had whipped up. She could now feel the coolness of the leather chesterfield against her bare arms. The flat though furnished in a solid British tradition, was strewn with signs of the stereotypical bachelor. The smell of fags and stale pizza hung in the air; a couple of empty beer cans lay on the carpet. Magazines and paper tossed wherever there was a vacant space.

Martina lay her head on Sam's shoulder for a cuddle. Loud voices were coming from the bedroom, the door half ajar.

"Crank the music up someone!" shouted Christian sticking his head out from behind the door; large aviator sunglasses firmly fixed to his face. Such a handsome face thought Martina as she reached for Sam's hand. The trip-hop track that was playing was turned up a notch. Someone from upstairs started banging on the floor erratically. It was 12.45 a.m. on the face of the imitation Big Ben clock standing on the mantle piece. People started screaming as they became excited. They waved

70

their arms in time to the music.

'Eeeeeeeeeeee!' A police siren spilled out into the night air.
…but no one could hear the warning above the music. Only the
pigeons sitting above the city rooftops were paying any
attention to what was happening. The terror that was to come.
The volume went up a notch. The party had gathered
momentum.

Martina turned to Sam, who had begun nibbling her ear; she
wanted to ask if he felt like dancing, only it wasn't Sam sat
next to her, but some stranger. Some stranger who she didn't
know from Adam. His eyes had a hunger in them.

"Get off me!" she yelled, pushing him off as she did so.

"Hey where's the fire sweetheart?" He pulled her back
towards him, his breath sour with gin.

"I said get off!" Martina pushed more violently, her hand
almost a fist in his stomach. She stood up and marched toward
the bedroom. None of the people she pushed by were Sam. She

pushed the door to the bedroom. Time seemed to have no place here. Her limbs froze. She felt like vomiting. Her stomach's contents now turning to quicksand. For the second time in her life she felt genuine shock. Felt that life had taken the earth from beneath her, taken away everything that she had put her faith in ..... just when she had begun to trust again.

There was Sam, sweet innocent Sam with his head bent over a mirror. Sweet innocent Sam who had whispered sweet nothings in her ear. Her rock. He looked up, white powder covering his top lip. "Martina!" He looked stunned, his eyes wide; a rabbit caught in head lights. She pulled the room door shut. WHAM! Sam on one side, her on the other. She ran into the kitchen not sure what to do.

"What's the matter Martina? You look as though you've seen a ghost." Kelly held a hand out to her friend, a bottle of Chablis in the other. "Martina?"

"It's Sam, he's in the bedroom and can you believe," her voice a slight edge to it – trying desperately to regain calm, "snorting cocaine, fucking cocaine!"

"Oh," Kelly had a look of concern but not surprise. She put the bottle down by the kitchen sink. "Let's take you home girl." She gave Martina a quick hug then went into the hall way to retrieve their jackets. Martina struggled to get hers on, her mind a confusion. "Here sweetie, let me help." The moment Kelly reached out, she collapsed into her, tears poured down her face. The tears hot to the skin; burning her cheeks. Inside she felt cold, lost, completely lost, the world made no sense anymore. And Kelly held her as her body trembled like a child who had been told daddy wont be living here any more.

*

Once inside the flat Martina flicked on the hall light and kicked off her heals. Her mind still spiralling. Her every move on autopilot. Kelly trailed behind her with one hand guiding her towards the bathroom in the small of her back.

"Come on darling," she said gently, "let me run you a bath". They entered the bathroom together. Martina stood in front of the mirror staring at her reflection. Momentarily in shadow, until her friend pulled the cord that flicked the light on. She recognised her body, but it could have been anyone's. She felt so empty, a familiar and sickening loneliness, just numb. Her mind continued to spiral, still trying to make sense of the nights events. Kelly moved her hand gently up onto her left shoulder as she slowly leaned over to kiss her, on the exposed area of neck above her collarbone. Something in her brain jolted. Not due to the shock of her friends actions, but the ease with which her body responded. She felt herself give way. Her emotions begin to recalibrate, her mind being rewired. She was feeling turned on. . .by a woman.

To Martina it seemed as though she was in a dream and this moment had already been scripted. Somehow pre-destined. How else could she explain the ease to which she turned around and kissed her friend full on the lips, the tip of her nose, and then the softness of her tongue entering Kelly's mouth. She felt herself returning…as though from a long and distant journey to arrive at this one particular point. Martina hesitated, 'what was she doing? What about Sam?'

'What about him?' said another much more urgent, more pressing voice. Light bounced around the room; Kelly's reflection revealing the beauty in her face.

It was as though for the first time she was seeing Kelly for what she really was. The luminosity of her delicate skin, allowing a steady glow to shine through. The radiance in her eyes a measure of her other worldliness, speaking without speaking. This was someone who had never let her down, had never judged her, never left without saying goodbye. Her thoughts spiralled back, just for a breath, to her parents. They had left – with no love you – no take care – and no goodbye. The tears were returning. Martina gulped, then moved around slowly. Her body starting to quiver; turning to liquid.

CHAPTER 8

Autumn was now firmly in control of the lottery that was the British weather. Greg had decided to wear a black sweat top from his wardrobe and a pair of black moleskin trousers. He sat at his drawing table sketching out different configurations for his bathroom project. He had decided to go for a Japanese minimalist concept under Charlie's influence. He had spent a couple of weeks during his last summer vacation, exploring some of the Buddhist temples in Japan. More like a pilgrimage he had called it. An awakening to his spirituality. He felt as though by some process of osmosis he had begun to be infused with the flavours, tastes, and sensibilities that he had brought back with him. He continued to make sketchy marks against the paper.

Belinda walked in; her hair harshly scraped back this morning, held in place by gel; a mug of steaming coffee in her hand. She walked gingerly over to Greg. He smiled inside, as he observed her desperately trying to keep the sweet dark substance from staining her wide flared slacks and tight cream fitted jacket. He knew the magnetism of coffee to anything cream or white.

"Morning Greg."

"Morning Belinda," his response polite.

"How are we getting on?" She looked over his shoulder, "Hmmm....describe this to me," she pointed to a couple of small squares sketched in next to what was clearly the bath.

"Oh that's an idea for a three stepped wall that is sculptural, but also functional as plinths for candles or towels."

"So in effect it's primary role is to screen the bath is it?"

"Yes but without loosing the openness that the space offers." Greg felt that he was talking like a designer now.

"Mmmm....that's great, I like it. But be careful to check your measurements, that bath looks rather big to me in relation to the rest of your room, okay?"

"Okay," Greg grinned, his slightly crooked teeth showing again, He felt relieved; she was pleased with what he had done. He was growing to like Belinda. She seemed to be softening, less rigid than before, less pretentious somehow. A more relaxed atmosphere followed her; her voice was less strained.

She moved on to look at the next person's work, while Greg got busy with his scale rule. He felt a cool breeze touch the back of his neck as someone pushed open a window. Hazy sunlight washing his paper anew. The door swung open and in walked Martina. She sat next to him, her face looked drawn and tired. The fine lines around her eyes looked more obvious…but somehow that only drew him closer, reminded him that she was only human…and that life left it's mark on everyone.

"Hi, you okay?" asked Greg.

"Not really," sighed Martina unable to lie.

"How about you?"

"A bit frazzled, I was working on this," he nodded at his drawings in front of him, "late last night. I really need to get cracking now. I still need to draw up my two elevations and a perspective for next weeks crit. Otherwise I'm chopped liver." He smiled at his friend but she didn't respond.

"I'm so behind," Martina's voice was low, "but…" her jaw dropped, "that's the least of my problems." She taped a sheet of tracing paper to the drawing board hastily.

"Anyhow, I had better get on with it." She tried to sound more upbeat, but failed.

" I'll buy you a coffee break time," Greg winked, "you can tell me all about it then."

Martina said nothing but smiled, glad of the invitation. Greg returned to his drawings, frantic now with the amount of work still left to do.

He could hear the student with Belinda ingratiating themselves sycophantically and groaned inwardly. Competition seemed rife on this course and quite a few of the students seemed to be using the ploy of bolstering the egos of both Belinda and Ben. Greg liked the fact that he had never seen Martina compromise herself for anyone, was never anything other than real. You either liked her or you didn't, that was the deal.

*

It was break time. Greg and Martina sat in the ultra modern refectory with it's chrome tables and bistro chairs. Blocks of strong colour on the walls. A slim designer sandwich sat on Greg's plate, thinly spread with what was described as cream cheese and chives. Greg chewed without interest.

"Jeees, this is dry as a bone." He opened out the sandwich to display it's contents to Martina. "How's yours?" She looked up, sweeping strands of her short brown hair back behind her left ear; her eyes a million miles away. Her face dead pan; it's mediterranean tone somewhat pale.

"It's Sam," she offered, her eyes lost and alone. Greg took her hand without thinking,

"What about Sam?" He felt her warm hand tremble beneath his. Felt her smooth skin and something inside took hold. He wanted to pull her close, hold her; protect her somehow. Smother her beautiful lips with kisses; be the one to take away the pain. What was this connection they had?

"Greg are you listening?"

"Oh sorry," he said suddenly releasing her hand. The connection gone. What was he doing? Charlie trusted him. He felt ashamed. What was he thinking? They were friends. He looked over at Martina, her face still dead pan, aware of a distraction but not the details, his momentary lapse. "Sorry, I'm listening." His voice soft, reassuring. He adjusted his position,

80

trying to focus on her sad watery eyes and what they were telling him.

*

As Greg arrived at Charing Cross station to make his transfer, he remembered that Charlie was coming over to his. He looked at his watch, 5.54p.m, he was already running late. Charlie would be at his flat for 6.30p.m. and he was always on time. He looked up at the platform indicator.

"Thank God," he sighed relief. The 5.50 to Lewisham station was running six minutes late from platform two. He ran.

'Beep, beep, beep!' went the doors as he launched himself into the first carriage he came to. He sighed again. He was on. Oh damn, he thought once sat down, out of rubbers, damn. Wonder if the co-op will have any or else the convenience store on the corner.' The type of shop that crammed everything into what he could only describe as a tardis.

At last, after what seemed an eternity the train ground to a halt at Lewisham station. It was 6.20p.m. and his flat was still a further fifteen minutes walk, ten at a trot. ' Skip the shopping list for now,' he thought, 'him and Charlie could come back out for that stuff later.' He ran flying down the high street.

"I've got a surprise for you ," said Charlie as he entered the flat, flapping a piece of paper in his hand. Greg kissed him lightly on the lips, pushing the front door shut behind them.

"Hmmm..I like surprises."

"Well hopefully you'll…" Greg gave his lover another kiss midstream, he felt impulsive, "like this." Charlie pulled back, his eyes shining. "I've written you a poem," he announced slipping out of his jacket whilst dropping onto the settee.

"…..that's really sweet," Greg felt a strange compulsion to blink, could feel his heart take a leap, pounding in his ears. He sat next to Charlie, a hand on his partners knee. "What's it called?" His heart still pounding.

"Exotic Fruit."

Charlie cleared his throat, before reading on, "Exotic fruit… is that what I am to you or is that what you are to me?

With your tongue you lick me up and down; with your warm embrace you peel me free.

Exotic fruit … is that how we are meant to be or is that what you see in me?

With my nostrils I breathe in your sweetness; with my moist skin I set your juices free.

Exotic fruit …is that how our passion is expressed or is that our vision of what could be?

With our tender touch we caress as one; with our open hearts we realise in a moment that the rhythm of love is always free.

Exotic fruit … is it a choice, a way to feel or a blessing we have been allowed to see?

With your energy rising, it's as if the sun has come down to me.

With your beauty, please set my spirit free.

Exotic fruit …exotic…fruit."

All thoughts of acquiring condoms, temporarily erased from Greg's mind. He was bowled over. Rendered speechless. White doves had flown from his heart. No limits in his head, just love.

He pulled his boyfriend to him, wrapping his arms around his body. Clung to him as though their bodies would melt into one. They sat like that with no words spoken, no utterance to describe the moment. Time drifted in and out, no longer the marker, no longer important…

Once more they had arrived at a new level of intimacy; this one greater than the last. Greg felt something within him open wider to the feeling, the growing expanse that negates but remains everything. That takes away the loss, the pain, the misery, the tears and the anguish. Makes it alright.

He was aware that neither of them had known their father. Too young, too irresponsible, they had both been told the stories, the tragedy of it all. It seemed no coincidence now, their coupling, this wound between them; their link to the past now subsumed by the present. Like a wave healing all in it's path.

*

It was 10.25p.m. when they left the flat, linking fingers as they walked down the high street towards the co-op. On entering their hands separated. Greg went over to the toiletry section whilst Charlie looked at magazines.

Baby oil, cotton buds, but no condoms. Greg sighed. He strolled over to Charlie's isle.

"No joy," he announced, his tone slightly peeved. "Convenience store it is then, yeah?" Charlie nodded returning his magazine to the rack. They paced the next fifteen minutes in silence before arriving at the small fronted shop.

They entered. An elderly black man was stacking Heinz Baked Beans onto a shelf in the middle of the shop. He looked up, already uneasy. He had seen couples like them before. Saw the intimacy between them as Greg absently reached into Charlie's trouser pocket for change. Before he had thought what he was doing, put his guard up.

"Hi, have you any condoms?" piped up Greg regaining his composure.

"Over there," said the man briskly, seemingly unsure as to whether he should be selling them such a commodity. After a few minutes, Greg ventured tentatively,

"Ah…please could you tell me, any lube at all? Only I don't see any." The man looked shocked.

"No." he said bluntly; almost reeling, as though such a question was unthinkable in his world. A world that simply seemed so far removed from the reality that was around him. There was no mistaking the signals. Greg knew they weren't welcome here. He became aware of a reggae track being turned up from behind the man's counter. Yes he recognised the lyrics okay…Boom bye bye in a batty man head. It was Buju Bantan the Jamaican DJ known for his homophobia and hysteria.

Once it would have been him, the old man behind the counter, looking for condoms, but furtively, secretly, in a time when sex was unspoken of, in this place he calls home. How ironic. Now it is them who are unwelcome; a second generation. Them who are the foreigners, in his land of false morality.

As usual Greg sat in meditation that night. Watching his breath move in and out. He counted one, two, three…till he reached ten then begun again. The incident with Martina came up into view, played itself out before him. He became the observer and the participant simultaneously. He breathed slowly and deeply, not judging, not grasping , just observing......then he prayed. Thanked God for his blessings, for sending him some one to love. A whisper of a smile crossed his lips. The choices one makes in being with another. The self sacrifice, the temptations, the agony and the ecstasy of it all.

CHAPTER 9

It had been two days and two nights since the party, and still no sign of Sam. The only communication a hurried message left on the answer service.

"This is BT call minder," said the electronic voice, " You have one saved message. If you want to hear it press one now. If…" Martina hung up. She had listened to Sam's message over and over again. Listening for a hint of remorse in his voice. Some indication that this had all been some terrible mistake. But no. Just a few words that gave away nothing.

"Look I need some time to get my head together Martina, but don't worry about me, I'm staying with a mate, Malcolm at the minute. I know we need to talk, how about Tuesday evening?" The machine stopped. Really it was a statement not a question – of course she would wait in this evening, of course she needed to talk; but with no return number little of the choice seemed to be hers.

Impatient , angry, confused, all kinds of emotions circled Martina's mind, but it was pain that tied them together; like a noose waiting to be pulled tight. Waiting for the air to be sucked from her. She watched the clock. Couldn't see how the relationship could continue, not now, not after what she had witnessed. She dreaded Sam's coming as much as she needed it. Needed to have this out. She would need to be strong. That's what the voice inside her head told her,

"You'll need to be strong girl." And yet she felt so weak – nerve endings tired from strain.

She looked down at what she was doing, the paper now covered in a series of rough organic shapes that had been rubbed out then pencilled in again. A low sigh escaped her lips. Some how all of this would need to be made good by the crit. With her mind so distracted Martina felt like giving up. But no, she couldn't, life demanded more.

The door bell went, ding dong. It was Sam, had to be Sam, couldn't be anyone else. It had gone nine o'clock; when evening goes into night. But he hadn't used his key.

" Sorry I'm late," said Sam sitting down at the kitchen table. "Got held up."

"Never mind," replied Martina trying to remain calm, "I'll get us a drink." She had gotten to the point of habitually brewing a pot of tea for the both them. She was at the sink before realising she was taking things for granted. The Sam who she had lived with before all this, took tea morning, noon, and night. She really couldn't be sure if this was the same Sam.

"Sorry did you want tea?" she asked, tea pot in hand.

"That's great," Sam replied hurriedly, not wanting too much delay on the proceedings. There was a formality in the air; both of them poised. Martina plonked down two mugs of steaming tea on the table, both unsugared. She sat down facing Sam, the sugar bowl between them.

"Thanks," said Sam, his eyes cast down. Any sign from her a possible stumbling block. "Look Martina…," he began, "I didn't mean for you to find out about my past the way you did."

"Your past!" Her eyes looked incredulous, her belly about to burst.

"One minute, hear me out." Sam kept his eyes cast down, his white wool hat crumpled up between his fingers. "My past... I hadn't touched drugs for a long time before the party. Long before I met you...I swear Martina". His eyes lifted slightly, darting up to her face then down again, her features unmoving. "I'm not trying to make excuses or say I'm proud of it, but you know I didn't have much of a child hood. Never felt much love. My parents were always working – never there much." His eyes filling like rock pools once more. There was a pause.

"Sure I did alright at college, but drugs took me out of myself, made me feel good again."

"What about yourself?" butted in Martina, "did drugs make you feel good about yourself, make you feel loved?"

"No," his forehead furrowed, he shrugged his shoulders, "just made me feel good, stopped me from thinking I guess, stopped me from feeling so damn lonely." He lifted his eyes once more. "I never had friends at college, not real friends. Everyone

91

thought I was boring, I thought I was boring. Drugs changed that …. For a while," His voice trailed off. His eyes cast down once more. "A part of me wanted to self destruct really; but I realise that now. Martina I care about myself now; care about us." His eyes were open wide now, speaking from the soul, wanting her to let him in again, to give him another chance. There was a momentary silence, the air thick and heavy.

"You know I would never have gotten involved with you if I'd known you've got a habit." Martina folded her arms.

"I know, but I'm not addicted, I swear, otherwise I'd have been deceiving you .. I know that." He continued looking straight at her, risking rejection. "M I love you. I wouldn't do anything to deliberately jeopardise our relationship," his voice pleading, Martina's face expressionless.

"Then what about the other night – that was cocaine for Christ's sake!"

"Martina listen to me, I got drunk, lost control. It won't happen again." Martina felt her lungs opening again, her heart pumping the blood around her body. "I've got you now, I don't

need drugs." Sam's eyes implored her to understand, to trust
him again.

"Why didn't you tell me earlier?" Martina felt confused. Her
mind dizzy.

"I didn't know how to," his voice cracked – close to tears.
"Didn't think I would need to I guess. Thought, oh I don't
know …I screwed up….I was afraid of how you would react. I
love you Martina." His eyes the eyes of a child, innocent,
afraid. And once more her heart melted.

"Sam," her voice weary, "have you ever injected?"

"No."

"Our relationship can't take anymore surprises; anymore
crisis." Sam reached out but Martina pulled back. "I mean it
Sam." He nodded. Tears trickled down both cheeks as she took
his hand. "There's something else." She held on tighter. "I slept
with Kelly the night.." Her voice trailed off. "Well the night of
the party. She felt Sam stiffen.

"You never told me you were bisexual?" Genuine confusion dropped like a fog over his eyes.

"I never knew myself...until now" She looked away, feeling guilty for not having known herself better.

Sam drew her too him. "None of it matters Martina, only that you still love me."

"I do." She said, as though he had just asked for her hand in marriage. And if he had she would have gladly given it. Life had brought them another way forward, where non had been before. Relief washed over Martina, cleansing her, reminding her that love could be strong, even when her body felt weak. They clung to each other there in the kitchen, motionless, another storm weathered. Exhausted, spent, but intact. Martina's eyes scrunched up. It felt as though the ground had left their feet. And this time she felt alive. Really alive.

*

The next morning Martina called Kelly. Sam had already left for work.

"It's all okay again Kelly. A minor miracle, but it's all okay."

"That's good to hear, you managed to talk things through."
Her voice even, understanding, motherly almost.

"A hell of a talk though. I tell you Kelly I was scared, scared
we'd have to separate ….. I'm serious about him Kelly."

"I know Martina, he knows that now. Maybe this is a test.
Maybe he needed to see how much you love him. How
committed you are."

"Yeah, probably your right. But I guess it's equally important
he know that I'd walk away if I had to. I'll do my best, but if
things aren't right I wont stay."

"That's all we can ever do is our best, isn't it sweetie?"
Martina let out a quiet sigh as she held the phone close against
her ear, feeling an almost imperceptible release.

CHAPTER 10

It was bright and sunny when Greg got up. A clear blue sky. Sure it was winter now, and for sure it would be chilly outside; but the sun shone. It seemed to say something about life, his life....

He had no money to speak of in the bank, only what was provided by his student loan and the occasional top up from his mum. He was scraping along the bottom of the financial barrel. But he was on a course that he loved, that stimulated him, excited him, and stretched him. So for him that made things okay. Love made things okay.

He thought of his relationship with Charlie, five months to the day. Sure they had the odd disagreement, but who didn't. He smiled to himself. Hated it when Charlie threw his wet towel on the bed after a shower, so, so irritating. Charlie called him fussy. "Stop being so bloody fussy," he'd say. He did have that flip side you often get with a fiery temperament. But then he could handle that. His nature was inclined to be much calmer.

"And you stop being such a pain in the neck." Same thing every time. His smile spread, they were a bit like an old married couple. The ones you see bickering over nothing, no malice or anything, just bickering.

Sure they had the lonely nights apart. Greg often busy with his technical drawings, Charlie pouring over the shop accounts evenings at his place. A phone call here and a quick coffee there. So it was mainly the weekends that they spent any real time with each other. Of course that created it's own tensions sometimes, but they talked things through. Found their middle ground. Compromise, wasn't that one of the most important things within a relationship? That ability to access some new part of yourself and yield to it for the benefit of another? At least that was Greg's take on things, that part of him that could be a brother, a best friend, and now a lover had taught him that. Yes, he could play all of these roles; if that was what life demanded of him.

Greg felt tired this morning. Dog tired. He had been up for half the night finalising his bathroom project; his eyes hurt from strain. Whatever the outcome of today's crit, he felt proud of himself, he had worked hard. He threw the duvet from his body, grabbed a towel from the airing cupboard, then climbed into the shower. His mind flooded with images of his lover beside him; there under the water with him. He closed his eyes as the warm water gushed onto his head and down his back, each drop pounding away, caressing him, stroking his skin, licking him clean. And there was Charlie smiling back at him, his cheeky grin. The water stopped as Greg switched the faucet off; suddenly aware of time passing.

*

They all gathered in the studio awaiting instructions from Belinda. She was clad in all blue today; a deep navy blue suit that was neatly hemmed in at the waist .

"Right Ben will be along shortly to help with your assessments, but in the mean time could everyone please get their sketch books and drawings out on the drawing tables. That way we can get around in a more organised fashion." Her

98

lipstick shone brightly. "We can use studio two also as there won't be enough space in here. At that moment her head spun round; in came Ben armoured in a thick tweed jacket, his mad curly hair looking wind swept. "We'll start with group A shall we Ben and work our way round ?" Ben nodded.

Everyone shuffled to find a table. Greg nudged Martina,

"At least we get it over with quickly." He smiled. She grinned a tired grin, the past months an imprint on her forehead.

"Sure thing," her voice lacking it's usual perkiness. Everyone else within the group looked tired. Greg guessed that he wasn't the only one who had spent the best part of the night working. He touched her arm empathetically. Just briefly, a warm friendly touch, before pulling his work from the portfolio. There was no charge between them now, no undercurrent. A line had been drawn invisibly in the ether; some sort of tacit understanding between them. He began sticking his pictures up onto the wall, neatly side by side. Bits of white tack separating between his fingers, until they were all up.

Belinda scrutinised Greg's bathroom plan with her ruler; looking closely at the line thickness. She asked Ben for a second opinion.

"Mmm," his lips pursed. "Definitely too thick but a nice conceptual style. I like this." He pointed to one of the other drawings.

"Yes," nodded Belinda, "a really nice perspective, I also like the use of colour." She turned to Greg, "Well done. A good first effort. We'll need to work on the line thickness' now, yes? And," she pointed to one of the lines on his plan, " this line doesn't quite look parallel to me." She turned to the other students, "Can you all remember to be very careful when re-working plans or other drawings, to line it up exactly as before. Greg has made a common error, one that we often see at this stage." She turned back to Greg. "Can we see your sketch book now?" She flipped through the pages breezily, apparently satisfied with his efforts. Ben nodded nonchantly before scribbling some remarks onto a piece of paper clipped to a board in his hand.

Greg breathed a sigh of relief. They moved onto Martina, her drawings now stuck to the wall.

'EEEEEEEE!' Briefly Greg glanced through the window as a car alarm went off across the street. The air seemed heavy somehow, laden with something that was intangible, something that was unsettling. Like a storm about to break. Who was to know.

'EEEEEEEEE!' He turned his attention back to the tutors.

CHAPTER 11

Martina watched as Belinda scrutinised her bathroom plan, measuring and dissecting.

"What material is this floor?" asked Belinda rather impatiently.

"Tiles," responded Martina slightly taken aback.

"Yes but what kind of tiles? They could be cork, wood, slate, anything!" Belinda's tone had become flippant and incredulous at the same time as though she were chastising a small child. Martina was incensed,

"You seemed fine with it when I showed you last class." She didn't understand, why was it that Belinda seemed hell bent on being so awful to her? Belinda enraged that she should be challenged, continued with no let up. She looked across the other drawings,

"Not enough detail here." She was shaking her head, pointing at the offending drawing. No encouragement seemed to be forthcoming and certainly none was in evidence, only each word more scathing than the last.

Had Martina inadvertently failed to read the signals, failed to play the game? Got off on the wrong footing? She couldn't figure it out. Why was she being singled out for such attack? The questions reeled around in her head. Had she made some dreadful faux- paux unknown to the uninitiated? Or had she shown herself to be unaffected by this strange new world where image is everything? And for some; pretension the currency to trade? Unmoved to ingratiate herself to those with the power? Was it this that was telling in her eyes, this that singled her out?

Martina didn't wait for an answer, simply left the room with Belinda and Ben staring at the open door.

*

Half an hour later and Martina was standing in Belinda's office, arms firmly across her chest. Belinda perched on the edge of her desk, looking baffled, her red lips perfectly made up.

"Now Martina we obviously have a problem," Belinda's words slightly tentative.

"You're a student here and I'm your tutor. You need to be able to take my instruction with out taking on, this, this defensive stance that you have." Martina kept her arms crossed non-the less.

"I'm sorry," she said firmly, "but I felt that the way you spoke to me was uncalled for," her voice was beginning to give way, "Criticising my work like that….." Martina's mouth felt dry. Her words drying up.

"Look, this is a highly demanding course and we haven't got time to molly cuddle people. It's my job to get students through the course. To push them." Belinda's eyes were blazing.

"Yes well maybe a little encouragement would be equally helpful." Martina found her footing again. There was a brief pause.

"Okay, I do take that on board, but trust me I do want you to succeed." Her tone had softened.

"Thank you," Martina felt herself begin to relax at this admission, needed to hear it on some level. Instinctively her arms began to unfold. A new dawning had finally arrived. That fuzzy indistinct blue pink light, where the horizon merges into day. A new respect lay bare before them. The air felt light once more. They smiled.

The following morning a white envelope arrived in the mail. It had the familiar red postmark of Chelsea College stamped in the top left hand corner. Martina fumbled with it ,then without opening it traipsed into the kitchen where Sam stood nibbling on a piece of toast, thick with jam.

"What you got there M?" His eyes were wide with interest, "looks interesting."

"Oh, I guess it must be the college telling me whether or not they're going to give me any money from the access fund. God Sam what am I going to do if …." Martina stopped, she knew that her panic button was being pushed and that she was worrying unnecessarily. She needed to open the envelope then take things from there. Her future was in the lap of the gods; she ripped it open. The contents of the envelope a mystery before her. Her breathing sounded laboured as she unfolded the stiff white paper. Her application had been successful. Her mind rushed. Euphoria swept through her. She had turned another corner. All was right in her world again. And the stream of life was flowing in the direction that she was meant to go. All she ever needed to do was trust. She was trying. She smiled at Sam. Felt like crying, but smiled.

Sam leaned across and kissed her silently on the lips. Love pouring into the both of them. Martina felt that time had stopped. Once more it had stopped. She savoured this; this feeling of oneness with all that life is and all that life can be.

*

Martina called Greg as soon as she had her breath back.
In half an hour they were both striding side by side along Dean street, on their way to Freud's basement bar for a celebratory coffee. They had both survived the first term; the first chapter in living their dream of becoming designers.

"Designers extraordinaire," laughed Martina throwing back her head; her sleek hair brushing the collar of her black fitted overcoat. Greg laughed back. His black roll neck and wide flapping wool coat a protection of sorts from the harsh wind that was whipping along the narrow streets that make up this

part of town. The sun was bright; but cold in the sky. For effect
Martina repeated, "We are designers extraordinaire … darling."
Putting emphasis on darling. "We are the darlings of Soho."
this time in a mock upper class voice. They both laughed again.
People were glancing over now … caught by the sudden surge
of infectious energy.

Martina felt like a kid. She grabbed Greg's shoulder suddenly
and twisted her body around to give him a quick hug. Then
pulled his arm as if to hurry him along.

"Wow … sure you need the coffee?" quipped Greg, caught
up in the headiness of it all. "Crikey might need something a bit
stronger than that, I'm thinking. You know Freud's do the best
Mohito's in town." He winked. Martina's red lipstick reflected
in the bright icy air…no sound came from her lips …just a
knowing nod and a smile. They heard the sound of a car stereo
blaring out in the distance. Hard core base pumped out…the
vibrations disappearing in the direction they had just come
from.

CHAPTER 12

Bring, bring, bring…… went the small black trill phone, bring, bring. Greg picked it up, still tired.

"Hello."

"Hi Greg," it was his sister Leoni, "How ya doing?"

"Mmmm, not bad, you know how it is, knackered from the crit yesterday."

"How did it go?" Her voice expectant.

"Yeah, pretty good. They seemed pleased with it all." Greg's tone of voice conveying his relief. "How are things on your end, things good at work?"

"Sure steady you know." Greg could feel his sister smiling on the other end. She loved her job, loved being in catering.

"How about mum and Bailey, are they good?"

"Sure, you know Bailey, still as busy as ever. We're like ships in the night at the moment. The Beeb have him working on some new programming. He seems really fired by this one, so you know,"

"He wants to make sure he rises to the challenge." Greg pitched in.

"That's right. Mum's good." Leoni giggled, " We went shopping over the weekend and picked out some new earrings. Get this, they're great with this new top I bought the same day so mum's agreed to give me the earrings."

"Leoni I don't believe you," Greg laughed, "always taking mums stuff."

"Well it's a mother daughter thing and she's still got great taste." They both laughed.

"How are you and Charlie getting on?" asked Leoni, traces of laughter still in her voice.

"We're still good; but we've …" his voice faltered, " been getting a bit worn out with the work schedule lately. You know how it can be."

"Oh sure," her voice even. "Everything else okay though?"

"Yeah…. I mean we're still good, but we've been hassled lately, you know when holding hands and stuff."

"What other stuff?" Leoni sounded more serious now.

"Well nothing else really, just holding hands."

"Mmmmm…I can imagine, your going to get that sort of thing from some type of people. What have they been shouting. The usual?"

"You got it.. queers and all that bullshit," Greg paused.

There was a silence for a moment, a dim humming over the telephone line.

"I mean it's crazy really," Greg resumed speaking, but now his tone giving away his anger, " We were just minding our own business, then next thing we're being fucking attacked." Greg could hear his voice breaking. "I feel like ….." A sadness caught in his throat, a weariness that he wasn't expecting.

"I know," replied Leoni sympathetically, her tone soothing. "it's not right is it?" she didn't wait for her brothers' reply but carried on, her words a soothing stream down the telephone cable, "I'm not sure how I would handle it if I was in your shoes. Guess you have to weigh up when and where you can hold hands…you know. Unfortunately the world's not always a fair place, is it Greg?" This time she paused.

"That's for sure."

"Reality aay?" Leoni's tone final, wanting to turn a corner in the conversation.

Greg sighed let something go.

"Too much reality sometimes," He said finally, his tone relaxed again. His sisters affection taking away the injustice of it all.

"Hey," Leoni piped up, "why don't you bring Charlie with you when you come down for the Christmas? She paused briefly, feeling things out, "We're all kind of curious to meet him, even Bailey." She laughed light heartedly.

"God it's that whole meeting the parents type scenario, that's kinda heavy isn't it, like taking the relationship to a whole other level."

They both laughed.

"Oh I think mum and Bailey might need a little more time before Charlie can start calling himself family ….. but I'm sure they'll give him their blessing once they see how happy he makes you," Leoni still light hearted. "Remember how mum was when I first took Craig home?"

111

"Oh God yes. Poor guy." They laughed now an easy bubbling laughter, there between them. Brother and sister.

"Thanks Leoni ," She always knew what to say. Greg knew that he was one of the lucky ones. He had a family who loved him...…

Charlie barely spoke to his family, usually at Christmas and birthdays. It was sad in a way, but he said it made him strong, more independent; he had learnt to love himself when others didn't know how. Said that they just couldn't accept it when he had told them he had fallen in love with another man. Things had been strained ever since. It could be different this year, thought Greg, he could enjoy Christmas with his family.

"I'll talk to you soon sis," said Greg, now out of his reverie, "send my love to mum could you; and a big hi to Bailey and Craig."

" Okay ,take care , don't do anything I wouldn't do." She teased.

"You take care too," He waited for Leoni to hang up. The line went click.

He rested the hand set back in it's cradle. Click.

*

The taste of strong, bitter coffee made Greg grimace slightly. A terms work had taken its toll. Though it was only early evening Greg couldn't stop yawning. He swilled down another mouthful of the bitter dark fluid, some missing his mouth and landing on his white cotton shirt.

"Oh shit!" he cursed. Suddenly alert as he panicked to undo the buttons and rinse the stain clean before it had a chance to dry on. The doorbell went, ding dong. It was Charlie on time as usual. They were visiting The Catacombs this evening on Martina's recommendation. She knew he loved central as much as her. Momentarily forgetting the spillage, Greg smiled to himself. He found himself thinking back to what had been said, they were the darlings of Soho. Rolled the words around in his mind. Liked the way they sounded. A feeling of friendship and affection rose up spontaneously like a wave out at sea, crashing several times before petering out against the shore. He made a mental note to give her a call very soon. He would treat her to coffee and pastry at Patisserie Valerie's, down on Compton Street. Images of her with head flung back, laughing at some shared joke, eyes lit up and bright, drifted past like clouds on a summers day. Ding-dong, went the bell again.

"Oh God, fashion crisis ," announced Greg as he opened the door now bare-chested, shirt in hand. He offered the evidence to Charlie as he entered.

"Oh no," grinned Charlie taking the offending garment, " we'll just have to stay in then won't we?" He winked, a glint in his eye.

"Not tonight Sir Lancelot," laughed Greg heartily, "I'm looking forward to a damn good nosh up." He folded his arms, "I want to be wined and dined." His eyes beaming.

"You'll be lucky, a bag of chips and a pickled onion; and that's your lot, alright?" Charlie joining in on the joke. Still laughing he pulled out his wallet and opened it. Peered inside. "Well that's going to have to be between us." He tried to look forlorn, but not quite making it sprayed his partner with saliva, laughing and stuttering at his own joke.

"Come on now, my treat." Greg pulled a plastic card from his pocket (dropping his shirt) and waved it in the air as though it were a flag. A cheeky grin stretched across his face.

*

When they descended the stairs to the restaurant they could hear the many chatting voices that wafted up to greet them. It was packed. Charlie whispered to Greg,

"Hey good looking do you think we'll get a seat ?" The hostess approached to seat them.

"Hi I've got just the seat for you." Her voice was like jade, smooth and translucent. Her hair hung in ringlets, long and shiny. She guided them over to a small table in an alcove not too far back, but not too far forward.

Tonight an elderly gentleman with white hair tinkled on the keys of the baby grand piano. The restaurant was alive with chatter and gaiety.

Greg admired the small red carnation in the vase in front of them while Charlie looked at the menu. He turned his head

115

suddenly aware of the gaze that was upon them. One couple smiled and Greg smiled back, holding them there with his eyes, just for a moment. He felt happy and giddy. 'What a funny life' thought Greg, a crazy beautiful life.

A life that never failed to show him some new angle. Some new way to fly as the spirit wants to. To love in spite of it all. And to grow as a consequence of being himself .... His eyes rested back on Charlie; his heart like a butterfly dancing to the tinkling of piano keys.

"I'm going for the goats cheese salad announced Charlie, how about you," he put the menu back down on the table.

"Mmmm.... Oh I think I'll have the same, and maybe a glass of house white to wash it down," Greg winked. "You up for some?" Charlie looked unsure. "Go ooon, lets celebrate.

"Celebrate what?"

"Us spending Christmas at my mum's place." Greg looked on amused; his partners brown eyes wide, speaking to him in a language that was familiar to him, without the need to say anything. It was another step forward for them. Another step together. And as they looked at each other in that way that couples do, there was the tinkling of the piano keys wafting on the air and a sweet bitter smell like dark mint chocolate.

CHAPTER 13

Exhausted from the last three months, Martina had given no thought to how her and Sam should spend the Christmas break. All she felt like doing was sleeping for the next three days and then some. She crawled under the duvet against Sam's soft warm body, leaned into his chest and rested there. She felt his arm behind her back pulling her to him.

"You okay darling, " he whispered.

"Mmmm….." She was too tired to formulate the words. She just rested there drifting off into sleep. A slow deep sleep that she could loose herself in, like a return to the womb. Some huge expance of nothingness. Her mind sliding, it was heaven. And then, there it was a nudge against her thigh. It was Sam.

"Honeeey," He pulled the word out in a, I'm feeling horny, are you kind of a way.

"Martina nuzzled her face under his arm pit. Course hairs against her nose. She pushed upward as though reaching for the surface of some great lake. Hoping to be rescued at shore. Cradled by the man she loved.

"Give us a cuddle, " Her voice groggy, eyes still shut. But no reply. Then it came again , the same thrust of the hips nudging her, coaxing her from sleep just yet. "I'm tired," she ventured, any interest in sex too far for her to reach.

Sam sat up switching the light on.

"What's going on?" he demanded, "you're on holiday so you can sleep in late, I'm the one who has to get up early."

"Honey it's late, all I want to do is sleep," Martina felt exasperated. It was she who couldn't understand what was going on." This behaviour from a man who not so long ago barely showed any interest in nocturnal stirrings. She turned away from him determined to sleep. But Sam wasn't having it.

"Don't turn away from me Martina. You haven't answered my question. What's going on don't you fancy me anymore?" This was getting silly. She couldn't believe what she was hearing. They had sex nearly every night. She sat up her arms folded, the light from the side table hurting her eyes. She took a deep sigh. "Look Sam can't we just cuddle anymore. What's the big deal, it's as though you're becoming obsessed. God gave you a right hand , why don't you use it if you're that horny?" Her tone was harsh. Martina had lost all patience, now angry at being kept awake.

Sam snapped the light off.

"Right, if that's your attitude." He made every effort to scrunch his body up to the edge of the bed. A trench down the centre of the bed. It was a strange slumber when Martina finally drifted to the world of dreams. Her body no longer seemed her own. There was a weird sense of floating in a strange dimly lit room where a man that she used to know had become her captor. She felt trapped. It was a fitful, restless slumber and the dawn seemed so very far.

It was late evening when Sam returned to the flat. Martina was in the kitchen chopping apples in preparation for an apple crumble that she was making. Simple things like baking were the sorts of things that she loved to do when she had the time. It always reminded her of her mother and the hours they used to spend in the kitchen together.

Her faded blue jeans were crumpled but that made her feel relaxed, some how more chilled out.

She looked over her shoulder. Tried to act naturally' half expecting last night to have been forgotten by now. Just a distant memory now in the freshness of the new day.

"Hi hon, good day?" Her short brown hair pulled behind her ears.

"Not bad," Sam sounded a bit grumpy not quite himself.

"Thought I'd bake us a crumble tonight, something a little different," Her voice trying to convey a need for harmony in the midst of her domesticity.

"Oh right." He dropped his bag heavily on the kitchen floor. His blond hair getting long was looking rough today. Uncombed. His chin unshaven.

Martina soldiered on determined to make last night a thing of the past, "I've left you some rice and a salad in the fridge as I wasn't sure what time you would get home tonight."

"Okay, thanks." His tone still set on mono. There was a strangeness in the air as an uncomfortable silence settled in the room. She continued to prepare ingredients. She had begun sifting flour into a bowl.

The silence was broken as Sam dragged a stool from under the kitchen counter and sat down.

"M ….." Began Sam.

"Oh by the way," interjected Martina I was wondering what you'd like to do with the Christmas break hon. I thought maybe we could visit Kelly, she always likes to have a couple friends over for a good nosh up." She tried to sound uncommitted, "though you know I won't mind what we do. Not really celebrated Christmas since, well you know since mum and dad passed on." Her voice dipped, she felt a little bit of sadness catch in the back of her throat. It still hurt sometimes. Half talking , half mixing with her hands, she tried not to look up. Not sure what else to say. The words seemed to fall against deaf ears. Sam merely sat observing, but saying nothing. "Are you thinking of seeing your mum at some point?" Martina's tone was searching , tenuous , careful not to sound as though she were inviting herself along. Unsure where she stood in the scheme of their relationship. Was meeting his mother something Sam wanted right now? Of course it was time but Martina wasn't sure anymore. Last night had made everything unsure. She looked up now. Stared Sam square in the eyes.

"We have to talk about last night ," he said flatly. His eyes no longer filled like rock pools. Something had changed. They had a glassy look to them, shielded some how from her view. No longer giving away their secrets. Barred and locked from the inside. Martina felt something deflate within her. Their relationship had steered into the rocks and she had been too tired to steer away. But it wasn't just last night. On hind sight this had been coming for days. Both of them to distracted by the everydayness of life to notice the course they had taken. Too complacent in the knowledge that sex had become the only way that they showed each other intimacy anymore. And now, now what?

Martina stopped her self from interrupting, Sam wasn't finished, she could see that. Scraping crumble mixture from her fingers, she pushed the bowl aside giving Sam her full attention.

"Look," he said, "don't you fancy me anymore, how come your not wanting me the way you used to?"

"Sam that's not the way it is at all. Because I don't want to shag for one night doesn't mean I no longer fancy you for goodness sake." Her tone was even, she tried to remain calm, adult like in approach.

"Well what's this about being tired, what about the times I'm tired and still we do it… must be almost every night. Basically how am I supposed to feel? I can't help wondering what's going on."

"What, because I don't want to have sex for one night, is this all our relationship rests on now? What's happened to you? Why are you so upset by one night?"

"Because I feel that it's …." He faltered. "I don't know, that you might be loosing interest in me. Being tired has never stopped us from having sex in the past."

"Sam ," Martina's voice gave away her exasperation, " Sam, sex isn't the end all and be all of our relationship is it? Gees. Some nights it would be just nice to cuddle, but you don't seem to be happy with that anymore. It's always got to be sex, well I'm sorry but I'm bored with that." There it was out. Something inside had given way. There was an edge to her voice. Sam opened his mouth but Martina wasn't finished she felt something inside pushing her on. "I'm not saying that I don't want to have sex with you Sam but now that you've raised the issue, I just don't want it on such a regular basis any more, I guess I need to use my energies in other ways. Needs do change within a relationship Sam and I guess that's what's happened, our needs have changed."

SILENCE

You could have heard a pin drop from next door, such was the stillness that followed. Perhaps they had reached a place of no return. Perhaps this was it. Out of nowhere they had found themselves at a precipice.

125

Sam stood up his head hung in thought for a second. His eyes searching his partners for some sign, some way back from the brink.

It was Martina who broke the silence,

"Look Sam I do love you and I do want to be in a relationship with you, but is there going to be room for compromise here?" Her voice sounded tired now, her energy dwindling. She waited for Sam's answer.

"Of course there is M. I guess I just needed to know that you still felt the same way about me, still loved me the same, you know?"

She reached out; her arms wide open. Once more they had found a way forward. Found a bridge to take them to the other side. She hugged Sam to her. Held him there in the centre of the room. Breathing but not breathing. Nothing between them, just love.

CHAPTER 14

Rocking back and forth, Greg and Charlie where making the soporific journey to Cambridge. They had left Kings Cross at 10.15a.m on the fast track and were due to reach Cambridge at 11.00a.m. It was now 10.30a.m. They sat side by side near the rear of the train where it was less crowded. Their hands intertwined, as Greg stared out of the window at the speeding landscape; a blur of greens and browns, the trees bare at this time of year.

EEEEEEEEEEEE! The train had entered a tunnel, Greg turned away from the window and smiled at his partner. His manner seemed slightly unsettled.

"You okay?" asked Greg, " not nervous or anything?"

"Mmmmm, maybe a little," admitted Charlie, "it's kind of that wondering what they'll make of me." He smiled, his shiny hair flopping over his forehead.

"Oh they'll love you," Greg's mouth stretched into a broad grin, his eyes bright, he paused, "I love you." The words sprang from his lips of their own volition. There it was, he had said it.

Said it out loud and he was glad.

Charlie looked like he was about to cry or laugh or both,

"I love you too," he said finally, his voice an almost whisper.
They sat there, playing with each other's fingers, and for a
moment the train seemed to contain only them. It felt strange.

"Hey," announced Greg pulling a piece of paper from his
pocket," I've got a surprise for you," he chuckled. "It's a poem
that I wrote last night." Charlie lifted his eyebrows in surprise.

"What's it called then?"

"A Crazy Beautiful Life." Greg paused for effect, before
carrying on.

In a moment I can fill you with wonder,
in the next a well of despair.

At times thrill you with new adventures,
And occasionally a beauty most rare.

EEEEEEEEEEEEEEEEEEEEE! They had entered another tunnel. In the dark their fingers intertwined once more, Greg's words lost for a moment as they hurtled towards their destination. Another chapter in the life that was before them. Suddenly plunged back into light, their journey had no limits, just possibilities as browns and greens merged together.

*

It felt weird being home again, his old home, with the familiar front door in traditional stained wood. The Yale lock ever so slightly stiff as it turned.

"Hello!" he announced stepping inside, "anybody home?" There it was the familiar smell, that he couldn't quite place. That vague hint of flowers and Sunday roasts. Charlie closed the door behind them tentatively as Lilly, (Greg's mother) called,

"In here!" from the kitchen. Leoni jumped up from her seat and,

"Mmmmmwa," went her lips as she kissed her brother on the cheek, "Hi stranger," she laughed, "God it's been ages."

"Hi sis," Greg kissed her back and gave her a squeeze round her waist. He then moved over towards the sink where his mother was drying her hands on a tea towel, her face beaming.

"Mmmmmwa, how's my baby?" Asked Lilly as she held Greg tight.

"I'm fine," his face a little sheepish, embarrassed at being hailed her baby in front of his partner. His partner who up to now was still standing in the kitchen door way, feeling slightly out of place, waiting to be introduced, not wanting to intrude on this reunion. Greg spun around, "Mum, Leoni, this is Charlie." He smiled reassuringly in Charlie's direction as Leoni made the move to take his hand,

"Hi," she said, squeezing Charlie's hand in her immediately familiar manner, her cherry coloured lips pulled into a radiant smile.

"Hi," he replied, letting his shoulders relax.

"Hello Charlie, nice to finally meet you," said Lilly moving across the kitchen to take his hand. Her manner a little reserved; still friendly, but a hint of holding back, of being not quite sure………

Steps could be heard coming down the stairs, a thud, thud, thud sound before Bailey came into join them, his ADDIDAS label blazoned across his chest. Greg introduced Charlie. He liked that his brother's manner was genial and friendly.

"What would you like to drink?" asked Lilly in her warm motherly way. Greg was home.

The day had turned into night and an overwhelming sense of calm had settled into Greg's brave new world. They all laughed and chatted and ate. Made merry as the first signs of snow drifted down from the sky's outside. Them cocooned in the warmth of family and affection. Tomorrow was Christmas eve, that would be a busy day, it always was. Greg always left the buying of his presents and cards till then. It was a tradition he enjoyed. Made his shopping more impulsive; so he told himself. He got up to show Charlie his room. His stomach did cart wheels as he got a strange sense of dejavu …there in his old room sat next to Charlie.

"Did I ever tell you," he turned to face his partner, his right leg up on the bed his left on the floor, "that one day whilst sitting here," he nodded to indicate the bed, "I had this experience ......he paused.... that within all of us is this endless stream of love, no beginning, no end, just love………………..

There was a silence, then,

"That's beautiful," said Charlie, his eyes shining against the light from the bedroom ceiling. "Greg I've been thinking," his tone somewhat tentative now, "how would you fancy living together....you and me?"

It was time again, time for another chapter in Greg's life to begin, his heart wide open he felt no fear. What ever was in store he would follow his heart.

EPILOGUE

Charlie heard the phone connect … it was ringing…

Greg answered almost immediately,

"Hi Charlie"

"Hi Greg" His voice tentative.

"Hi Charlie….love you."

Charlie's voice was low, relief washing over him.

"Thank God…So good to hear your voice…are you both okay? I've been trying to call ever since I heard…."His voice stopped ..no longer under his control … his emotions finally giving way. . there was just silence as Greg continued to hold his phone to his ear.

"Martina's here with me …we're both fine …the darlings of Soho…just shook up. I love you…Martina's saying hi…Charlie you okay?

"Yeah … yeah …sure ..just so good to hear you….love you too."

Greg felt his nerve give way and held onto Martina….there by the road side, directly out side of Kings Cross station. The air still heavy with the sickening smell of smoke; the uncontrollable crying all around them; the sobbing; the shaking. The automated voice repeatedly telling people to evacuate; sirens screaming. He held onto Martina…and she held onto him. There by the road side. Each of them some how changed. Moved that there was still love in the world.

David Barnett is the author of 'An Alien By Circumstance,'

published 1996 by Minerva Press.

He studied in Cambridge for some years before moving to

London to become a teacher. It was whilst training that he

begun his first novel. This has gone on to be sold both in the

U.K. and in America, as well as being broadcast on the BBC

radio.

He currently lives and works in London.

2451987R00072

Printed in Great Britain
by Amazon.co.uk, Ltd.,
Marston Gate.